The Picture of D
A Gay No
By
Mark A. Roeder

The Picture of Dorian Gray
A Gay Novel
© 2011 Mark A. Roeder

Cover Photo Credit: Eduard Stelmakh on Dreamstime.com.

Cover Design: Mark A. Roeder

ISBN-13: 978-1466478411

ISBN-10: 1466478411

All Rights Reserved

Printed in the United States of America

Acknowledgements

I'd like to thank Ken Clark and James Adkinson for all the work they put in proof-reading this book. Without their dedication this book would be an unreadable disaster.

The Picture of Dorian Gray is, among other things, a story of depravity and moral decay. When Oscar Wilde wrote his tale in the nineteenth century, he could not go too far in the telling. In seeking to tell the story in manner I believe Oscar Wilde would have told his tale, had he dared, I have been forced to cross lines I usually do not cross. Those who read my novels are accustomed to what I call my "Alfred Hitchcock Approach" to sex scenes, wherein I provide just enough information for the reader to fill in all the details. Some of my novels include more explicit scenes than others, depending on the needs of the story. *The Picture of Dorian Gray* is a tale that requires sexually explicit scenes, if it is to be told properly, and is therefore not a tale suitable for younger readers. If you are offended by graphically sexual situations you should not read this book. That said, this is not an erotic novel. There is far more story than sex here. As with all my novels, I include sexual situations only as they are needed. It is just that what is needed for this story is more intense than usual.

Introduction

I have always wondered what Oscar Wilde would have written if he was not confined by Victorian standards of morality. Oscar Wilde pushed the boundaries both in his writing and his personal life, but even so the standards of 1890 were quite different from those of today. I have endeavored to write Wilde's tale as he would have done had he dared. In doing so, I'm pushing the boundaries of my own writing standards and the standards of morality of my time. Perhaps I would be more correct in saying that I have endeavored to write Oscar Wilde's tale as he would have done if he lived in twenty-first century America.

I have stuck with Wilde's basic tale only. The further one reads, the more my story diverges from the original. After all, what is the point of making a copy of what already exists?

Table of Contents

Chapter One: A Devil's Bargain

Bloomington, Indiana
Summer 1982
Seth

I stood gazing at a portrait of the most beautiful youth I had ever beheld. The painting was nearly life-size and its subject was of such exquisite beauty I wondered if he was real or some idealized fancy of my acquaintance's imagination. Daulton was known for his love of beautiful youths, not that he would do anything improper. He was too timid, reserved, and moral to do any such thing. I had no such reservations.

"It is the best work you've ever done, Daulton. You must exhibit it in New York, Los Angeles, or at the very least Chicago. Bloomington has some excellent art galleries, but this...this belongs where it can be viewed by a multitude."

"I do not plan to exhibit it anywhere."

"You must! It will establish your name in the art world. Someday, quite soon I think, this piece will hang in one of the great art museums of the world."

"I cannot allow others to see it. I would not have let even you view it had you not surprised me with your visit."

"Why?"

"I've put too much of myself in it, Seth."

"It looks nothing like you. I'm not knocking your appearance, Daulton. You're a handsome young man, but you look nothing like this blond Adonis."

Blond Adonis indeed. The boy on the canvas was youth perfected—his blond hair, blue eyes, perfect complexion, beguiling smile, and sensual, youthful body were the very ideal of young manhood. This boy of no more than eighteen was so beautiful I could not take my eyes from him. No wonder he had so captured Daulton, if he was indeed real.

"You do not understand, Seth. Of course I don't look like him! I am twenty-eight. He is eighteen. I am ordinary-looking. Dorian Gray is beautiful."

"Dorian Gray? So that is his name."

"Yes, but I did not mean to tell it to you."

"Why not?"

"Because I do not wish you to corrupt him."

"Corrupt him?"

"Yes, with your indulgent life-style."

"You have too little pleasure in your life, Daulton. You would be happy if you followed my philosophy, but go on, explain what you mean. How does this painting of someone else reveal too much of you?"

"Every portrait that is painted with feeling is a portrait of the artist, not the sitter. It is the painter who reveals himself. I am afraid I have put so much of myself into this painting that I have revealed my own soul."

I gazed at the painting.

"I see an extraordinarily beautiful youth at the very beginning of manhood. I see a face and form that will inspire envy in anyone who views them. I see nothing of you, Daulton, except your talent, which is more evidently extraordinary than even I guessed and you know I possess a true appreciation for your work."

"I knew you would not understand, but you have caught a hint of what I mean. Do you remember the landscape I did of Cascades Park; the painting I would not sell even though I was offer four-times my usual price?"

"Yes, it was magnificent."

"It was magnificent because I painted it with Dorian Gray at my side. He is my muse. With his inspiration I feel that I can do anything. He was completely transformed my art."

"You are obsessed with him. I must meet his young man."

"No, you must not."

There was a knock at the door. Daulton checked the time and the horrid look on his face told me exactly who was at the door. Daulton looked at me a moment, started to speak, then closed his mouth. The knock repeated and Daulton answered it. In moments, I was face-to-face with Dorian Gray. He was every bit as exquisite and beautiful as his portrait.

"Dorian, this is my friend, Seth Wotton. I'm afraid he'll be unable to stay."

"I can manage a few minutes," I said, easily dodging Daulton's attempt to rid himself of me. "It's very nice to meet the young man who inspired such an incredible portrait. I must admit I couldn't decide if you were real or a product of Daulton's imagination, but I can see you are no illusion."

Dorian was every inch as beautiful as his portrait, with his finely curved scarlet lips, frank blue eyes, and flowing golden hair. There was something about his face that made one trust him at once.

Daulton was busy mixing his colors for the portrait, as incredible as it was, was not finished in the painter's eyes. I could not for the life of me see what remained to be done, but I was not a painter.

"Seth, I would like to finish Dorian's portrait today. Would you think it terribly rude of me to ask you to go away?"

"Oh, please don't go, Seth. I can see that Daulton is in one of his sulky moods and I can't bear him when he sulks," Dorian said. "Besides, he never speaks while he is painting and it's horribly boring just standing and trying to look pleasant. I also want to find out if you're really as bad an influence as Daulton says."

I looked at Daulton for a moment.

"You didn't tell me you'd been talking about me." I turned back to Dorian and smiled.

"There is no such thing as a good influence. To influence someone is to change him. He no longer thinks his own thoughts and even his sins are borrowed. He becomes an echo of someone else."

Dorian grinned.

"Stay then, Seth, and entertain Dorian while I paint," Daulton said.

Dorian stepped up on a small platform and stuck the pose in Daulton's painting.

"So you think all influence is bad?" Dorian asked.

"The aim of life is to truly live up to one's nature. I believe that if a man were to live out his life fully and completely, were to give form to every feeling, expression to every thought, and reality to every dream—I believe both he and the world would gain a true state of joy. The only way to get rid of a temptation is to yield to it. Resist it, and your soul grows sick with longing for the forbidden. You, as young as you are, Dorian, have had desires and thoughts that have filled you with terror, dreams that make you blush with shame."

I watched Dorian as he posed in silence, deep in thought. I knew not to speak, but to let my words sink in. Daulton spared me a look of disapproval. His very expression said, 'Do not corrupt the boy.' Both Daulton and I knew that I already had. I had unleashed an idea that would consume him.

Daulton painted away for another hour. When he began I could not see anything that need be done to the painting, but I admitted to myself that it was growing more life-life and real. I almost felt as if the Dorian in the portrait could speak to me.

"I need a break, Daulton. I can't stand here a moment more," said the beautiful boy.

"Sorry, as you know I lose all track of time when I'm painting. Why don't you go for a stroll in the garden?"

"I'll go with you," I said. Daulton looked as if he was about to object, but then sealed his lips and went back to his work.

Since Daulton was occupied, I fixed Dorian and me glasses of iced-tea and carried them into the garden. Dorian was leaning into the honey-suckle, sniffing its sweet, delicate scent.

"Thank you," he said, taking the iced-tea I offered.

"You should get out of the sun. With your fair skin you'll burn."

"What does it matter?"

"It should matter everything to you, Dorian. You have the most marvelous youth and youth is the one thing worth having."

"I don't think so."

"You will, one day when you are old, wrinkled, and ugly. Now, you can charm the world with your youth and beauty, but will it always be so? You have only a few years to live perfectly and fully. When your youth goes, your beauty will go with it, and you will have to live with mere memories of your glorious past. Time is jealous of you and will seek to destroy you."

"Do come back in will you?" Daulton asked from the open door. "The light is perfect now. You can bring your drinks."

Dorian returned to his pose and I sat alternating watching him and watching Daulton at his work. It simply amazed me that anyone could create beauty with paints and a few brushes.

After about fifteen minutes, Daulton stopped, stepped back, and examined his work.

"It's quite finished," he said, then leaned down and wrote his name in the left-hand corner of the canvas.

I stood and gazed at the painting.

"Congratulations. It is the finest portrait you've ever painted."

Dorian came and gazed upon his portrait. The sense of his own beauty came to him like a revelation. He had never felt it before. Only at this moment when he viewed himself through the eyes of another did he understand that he was really and truly beautiful.

Dorian frowned and I knew exactly what he was thinking. His eyes told the tale just as they did his suddenly awareness of his beauty. He looked as if he might cry.

"Do you like it?" Daulton asked.

"Of course he likes it. Who wouldn't like it? It is the greatest work of art in modern times, perhaps in all times. I will give you anything you ask for it. I must have it," I said.

"It is not mine to sell. It is Dorian's," Daulton said.

"You are extremely lucky, Dorian," I said.

"How sad it is!" Dorian murmured. "I shall grow old, and horrible, and dreadful, but this picture will remain always young! It will never be older than it is this day. If only it were the other way! If it were I who was to be always young, and the picture that was to grow old! For that I would give everything! I would give my soul for that!"

"Daulton would not like that," I said.

"Indeed not. It would truly ruin my work."

"You like your art better than your friends," Dorian said angrily. "I am no more to you than that your bronze Hermes or your silver Faun. No, I am less. How long will you like me? Until I have my first wrinkle? Your picture has taught me that Seth is perfectly right. Youth is the only thing worth having. When I begin to grow old I shall kill myself."

"Dorian don't talk like that," Daulton said.

"Why did you paint my portrait? It will mock me every day!" Dorian began to cry.

"This is your doing, Seth," Daulton said. "You should have gone away when I asked you."

I fought the smile that struggled to form on my lips, only partly succeeding. Dorian was in a horrible state. His tears would not stop.

"I will not allow it to mock you," Daulton said, picking up a small knife from his pallet. He walked to the canvas. He was going to destroy it.

"Daulton, don't!" Dorian cried, throwing himself in the way. "It would be murder!"

"I am glad you appreciate my work at least," Daulton said.

"Appreciate it? I am in love with it. It is part of myself. I can *feel* it."

"As soon as it is varnished and framed it is yours. I shall have it delivered to your place," Daulton said.

Daulton made us some hot tea and we sat down at a small table and talked. Daulton kept shooting me disapproving glances, but Dorian gazed at me with respect He knew I had revealed a truth to him—a truth that would forever change his life.

Chapter Two: First Conquest

Dorian

I sat at a table outside the Scholar's Inn Bakehouse and watched passersby. More than a month had passed since Daulton had finished the portrait, my portrait, that was now hanging in my hotel room. I had seen little of Daulton, but much of Seth. The older man intrigued me with his wisdom and view of life. He was correct, the only thing that truly mattered was youth. I could see it in the eyes of those who gazed at me as they walked by. They were as enslaved by my beauty as Daulton had been on the day we met.

Yes, I have grown conceited since the day my portrait was finished, or rather I became conceited on that day. Youth is the time for conceit and I felt no shame in it. Each of us had only so long to be young, beautiful, and conceited.

The other students were beginning to arrive and Bloomington was coming to life. I was eager for my freshman year at Indiana University. I was eager for the parties and the sexy boys I intended to seduce.

I was glad I'd met Seth. He had introduced me to so many new experiences. Most importantly, he had taught me with actions what he had taught with words on the day we met. The aim of life is to live up to one's nature. The only way to free oneself from temptation is to yield to it. I had fought my nature and temptation all through high school, but here I would be a new Dorian. I would be the Dorian I was truly meant to be. I was young, rich, and beautiful and I intended to enjoy all three while they lasted. This was my time and I was going to make the most of it.

I finished my lunch and then walked back to the Hilton Garden Inn, which had been my temporary residence during the summer. At last, I could finally get into my dorm. I had managed a large private room in Read. It was actually a suite meant for three, but I'd pulled several strings to get it all to myself. The cost was considerable, but the fortune my parents had left me was inexhaustible.

I packed up the reminder of my clothing and stopped to gaze at my portrait. Sometimes, when I looked at it, I felt as if I was looking into a mirror instead of looking at a painting. I almost expected myself to speak to me. The painting was too large for my Jag so I'd arranged for movers to deliver it to my dorm room. I gazed at the painting once more, then picked up my bags and carried them out to my convertible.

It was a short drive to Read, which was located near the corner of Third Street and Jordan. I had scouted it out during the weeks I'd lived in the Hilton Garden Inn. I was going to miss the maid and room service, but I wanted to be on campus. I wanted to be in the thick of the action and I couldn't do that living aloof in a hotel. I was willing to sacrifice some comfort for fun and I intended to make my suite as luxurious as possible. Besides, freshmen were required to live on campus.

I parked the Jag, grabbed a couple of bags, and walked inside. I examined my room assignment and made my way to my suite. I found it easy enough and let myself in with my key.

The suite certainly wasn't a luxury hotel, but it would do. There was a large open living-area with a nice view. There were three separate rooms, all small, but livable. One I would use for a bedroom, another as a study-area, and the third...I'd decide on that later.

The carpet was in a dreadful state and the rooms were empty. No matter, I could take care of that easily enough. I was not the typical poor college freshman. In a few days' time at most there would be new carpet on the floor and new furnishings. I refused to live in squalor.

I could hear students passing in the hallway, moving into to their own rooms. I smiled. Yes, this is what I wanted, to be surrounded by others my own age. I had enjoyed Daulton and particularly Seth's company during the summer months, but both were older, in Seth's case much older. Daulton worshipped and desired me. I enjoyed his attentions and flirted with him horribly. I fear I might have driven him near insane with longing and desire at times, but even so he was thankful for any scrap of attention I threw his way. I was a bit bored with him, but I couldn't dislike someone who so worshipped me. I did not intend to discard him completely now that I was soon to have friends my own age. No, Daulton intrigued me, and Seth even more so.

I made a few trips to the Jag for my things, which were mostly clothing, shoes, and small personal items. Everything else I intended to buy. I had already purchased a bedroom suite, which was due to be delivered at two, the same time as my painting was scheduled to arrive from the hotel. I had time to spare so I strolled around, passing first University Apartments West and East, then Forest Quad. The air was filled with a sense of excitement and anticipation. Everywhere college students were carrying boxes, suitcases, and bags from cars into their dorms. I lingered near Forest to watch an especially handsome and built boy with light brown hair open the door of a Cutlass Supreme. He bent over to pull boxes from the back seat, displaying the hottest ass. I felt myself hardening on the spot. When he stood, his muscles bulged under the weight of a heavy box. I glanced around to make sure no one was watching me as I watched him. The young hunk placed the box on the top of his car, while he pulled out two more boxes. He balanced the whole lot and then walked toward Forest. Just as I was ready to continue my walk and cease ogling his flexing pecs and biceps, the top box slid off and hit the ground.

"Need a little help?" I asked, quickly moving in.

"Please," he said with a smile.

I picked up the box and place it on top of the stack.

"Thank you..."

"Dorian. You're welcome."

"I'm Brendan."

I had an overpowering urge to lean in and kiss him, but with his bulging muscles he could easily snap me like a twig. Still, he was too sexy to resist. I leaned in and...

"I'd stay and talk, but this is rather heavy. Thanks again."

The moment was gone, I'd waited a fraction of a second too long. I gazed at his broad shoulders and hot ass with longing as he walked away.

I smiled as I continued on toward past Forest and turned left. I had not kissed buff and beautiful Brendan, but I had tried. Seth was right. The whole point of life was living up to one's nature. I would never have dared such a thing as kissing a complete stranger before I met Seth, but now I most certainly would... indeed had. The fact that I failed meant nothing. I had leaned into toward Brendan with the intent of kissing him. The next hunk who crossed my path would not escape so easily.

I passed the three Wiley Dorms on my right and turned left again in the direction of Read. I checked out the other college boys as I strolled along. They came in all shapes, colors, and sizes. I began to wonder how many of them I could, and would, have before the end of the school year. My body burned with desire and I had every intention of indulging myself.

It was near two when I arrived back at Read so I waited outside and watched yet more college boys unpacking their cars. More than a few took note of me. I flirted with the sexier boys, but at the moment I was just window shopping.

There were girls unpacking as well, but I cared not at all for them. Girls had never interested me much. They were okay as casual friends, but as anything more...no. Almost without exception the girls took note of me, but I didn't flirt or encourage them in any way. I was pleasant when spoken to, but nothing more.

The delivery vans from both the hotel and the furniture store arrived almost together so I was able to show the workmen from both to my dorm room with a single trip. I instructed the men from the Hilton to place my portrait upon its easel in the room I'd set aside for studying. The framed painting had been wrapped in plain, brown paper for its short trip, but I could feel its eyes gazing at me none-the-less. I tipped both the hotel employees with a twenty and then went to check on the men from the furniture store.

The two men were setting up my full-sized bed. A single would not do for this college boy. One of the men was quite young, only a couple of years older than me, and quite attractive with his dark hair, brown eyes, and tanned skin. He wasn't as buff as Brendan of Forest Quad, but his chest and arms bulged against his shirt in all the right places. After I entered the room he had difficulty in keeping his eyes on his work instead of on me. With one look into his eyes I knew I could have him if I wished. I smiled at him seductively and derived intense pleasure from the look of longing mixed with embarrassment that crossed his handsome face.

I felt myself hardening as I fantasized about pushing the older hunk to his knees and thrusting my crotch into his face. From his blush I guessed he had a girlfriend or wife and wasn't comfortable with his desires for other men. Perhaps he'd never experimented, but some part of him yearned to be with another man. It would take only a push...

"I'm not sure we have the right side-board. It should fit better than this. I'll have to call the store," the older man said and departed.

This was my chance. I walked over to the uncomfortable young man who tried and failed not to gaze upon me with longing. I closed the distance between us until we were mere inches apart. I stared into his eyes, reached out, and ran my hand over his crotch. He was rock-hard.

I ran my hand up over his firm torso and gripped his shoulder, pushing him down. He resisted only slightly before he dropped to his knees.

He wasted no time, for we had no time to waste. His fellow workman would return all too soon. He tore his way through my belt, button, and zipper and engulfed me.

I moaned as he drew me into his mouth and let him work his magic. I gazed down at him and watched as he served me on his knees. My lips curled in satisfaction and disdain. I gripped the sides of his head and thrust into his mouth. I held his head in place while I used him. He struggled only feebly and soon surrendered his mouth to me completely. I thrust with thoughts only of my own pleasure. In a few moments I moaned loudly and felt my orgasm rip through my entire body.

When I finished with him, I pulled up my pants and fastened my belt. He stood, looking more embarrassed than ever. A short laugh escaped my lips as I gazed into his eyes. He looked away awkwardly, too uncomfortable to maintain my gaze. His partner returned soon, entirely unaware of what had transpired in his absence. The younger man, whose name I had never asked, looked as if he feared I might say something to give him away. I could read the fear in his eyes. I smiled at him mischievously and then left the room.

When the pair departed, my bed, mattress, dresser, and two side tables were in place. It would all have to be moved when my new carpet was installed, but there would be men to take care of that.

I knew my schedule would soon be hectic and I was one for getting things done so I locked up, walked to my Jag, and headed for the eastside, which was all of a three-minute drive. I stopped at the first furniture store I spotted and walked inside, ready to make some salesman's day.

I headed for the small area dedicated to carpet first and flipped through the samples. Beige, light beige, dark beige—there was far too much beige in the world. I kept looking and then I spotted it, Indiana University crimson. I quickly made arrangements to have my suite measured and the carpet laid as soon as possible.

I moved next to furnishings. My bedroom suite was already in place, but I needed a couch, end tables, a comfortable chair for reading, a kitchen table and chairs, bookcases, and various other furnishings. I think the salesman was a bit skeptical when I walked through the store pointing saying "I'll take that and that." His skepticism quickly ended when I whipped out my American Express and my purchase was quickly approved.

I had to immediately return to Read to let in the store employees who were coming to measure for my carpet. Spending hundreds of dollars made me a priority customer.

An hour later, I was alone again. My carpet would be laid the very next day and the furniture delivered as soon as the carpet was down. My living space was coming together nicely.

I walked back outside. I was too excited to stay in my mostly empty suite. There was a great hustle and bustle all over campus. The morning had been active, but now it seemed that everyone was moving in all at once. I was amazed at the number of good-looking guys. I liked a variety of types, from slim to built. IU was like a buffet and I intended to fill my tray with hot, young men. I grinned when I thought of the workman I'd pushed to his knees earlier. Yeah, I was going to enjoy college life!

As much as I eyed the sexy college boys around me, I was eyed even more. Guys, girls, young, old—they all checked me out. One boy's father practically bored holes in me with his eyes as he helped his son carry a trunk inside. I knew I could have him if I wanted him. He was good looking for an older guy. His son was hot, with dark red hair, and a nicely muscled body he showed off by wearing a tank top. I fantasized for a moment about having both father and son, then winked at the dad and walked across the street toward University Apartments East.

I had thought there was plenty of activity in Bloomington during the summer, but I had been so very wrong. It was as if the population had suddenly increased ten-fold in a day. For all I knew, it had. I strolled up to Forest Quad, hoping to get another look at Brendan. I should have asked him out on the spot. True, he likely wasn't sexual interested in guys, but if he was straight it would have only made seducing him that much more exciting.

I did not see Brendan, but there was plenty of eye-candy about. Yeah, I was going to love IU. I just hoped I'd find the time to study.

Chapter Three: Caleb Black

My days leading up to the first day of classes were filled with parties, drinking, and spontaneous sexual encounters. I'd made out with an incredibly hot frat boy on a couch while those around us drank themselves into oblivion. At another party, I slipped away to a bedroom with a boy/girl couple who took turns making out with me. I wasn't much into girls, but I was into kissing her while her boyfriend watched. I was even more into the two of them taking turns giving me head. At yet another party, I'd gone down on a very straight, very horny, and very drunk jock who was on the varsity wrestling team. He'd resisted me, but once I got my lips around him he was mine. He jerked his pants up and hurried away after he'd finished. I grinned with the satisfaction of seducing a straight boy.

I took a moment to admire my suite before departing for my first-ever college class. The crimson carpet breathed life into what had been a sterile place. The comfortable leather sofa and club chairs made my suite look like no other college dorm. Works of art painted by Daulton graced the walls. One was of the Dunn's Woods on campus, which was one of my favorite spots. Another was of Daulton's garden in spring, with a profusion of daffodils and tulips. I'd purchased the biggest and best television available as well as a VCR and a microwave oven. I had little doubt mine was the most comfortable suite on campus.

I grabbed my backpack and headed out for my first class. I had two back-to-back classes in the morning with just enough time in between to get from one to the other without hurrying. My first class of the afternoon wasn't until 2:00 so I had plenty of time for a long lunch or whatever or whoever I felt like doing.

I eagerly anticipated my afternoon class. While most of my schedule was filled with freshman level required courses, my afternoon course was Theater 121: Acting for Majors. Theater was a passion of mine. I loved plays. I loved actors. I had performed in high school and I wasn't bad. I had no delusions about becoming a great actor, but success was unimportant. I had inherited a large stock portfolio from my parents as well as enough money to last me forever. Financially I was set and that gave me the freedom to do whatever I wanted with my life. I loved the whole world of theater and I wanted to be a part of it. I want to be around the actors. I wanted to work near the sets and the lights. I wanted to immerse myself in the world of the stage.

The class met in what amounted to a small theater, with raised seating, a small stage, and even stage-lighting. There wasn't enough room to put on any kind of real production and yet the classroom was enough like the real thing that my heart began to beat a little faster.

There were some thirty-five students, which was good news. I'd feared there might be well over two-hundred as there had been in one of my morning, freshman-level courses. While I had no great dreams of becoming a star I did want to become the best actor I could.

I sat there with my crisp, new text book in my lap, smiling to myself about the girls and guys who kept checking me out. I wasn't too surprised that the boys more openly gazed at me here. The theater was well-known as a haven for gays. It was a stereotype, yes, but one that held fairly true. One particularly handsome boy who was so small and thin he looked as if he was fourteen could not keep his eyes off me. I looked toward him and winked. He immediately turned as crimson as my carpet.

It was at that moment that Caleb Black entered my world. I did not yet know his name, but the moment I set eyes on him I knew he would change my life forever. He was handsome to the point of being beautiful, with curly black hair, emerald eyes, and full red lips. It was his good looks that I noticed, but it was his talent on the stage that was soon to draw me to him. There were plenty of good-looking guys at IU and while Caleb was very good-looking there were others still more attractive. Our eyes met for a moment and then he took a seat near the front.

I could see only the back of Caleb's head, but I felt drawn to him. For the moment, I paid more attention to the blushing blond boy. He was quite cute and even sexy in his way. I decided that I would have him, today perhaps.

Professor Sutton entered the room carrying a valise and a disorganized stack of what I guessed were scripts. He was in his late-30s, rather handsome, with a trim body. Hmm, perhaps I'd have him too. There were so many guys to seduce... and so little time.

Professor Sutton handed out a syllabus, which was heavy on reading, but I was delighted when our professor announced that he intended to spend little time lecturing and would concentrate on hands-on exercises. He made it clear that this was not an easy course and we would be tested heavily on our reading assignments.

Professor Sutton threw us directly into acting. He handed out scripts, no two alike, and informed us we would take turns upon the stage. We were to concentrate on voice projection and bringing the character to life. I thumbed through my script during the time allowed, trying to decide what I could find in Christopher Marlow's *Doctor Faustus* to perform. I decided on the famous section that began: "Was this the face that launch'd a thousand ships, and burnt the topless towers of Ilium?—Sweet Helen, make me immortal with a kiss." The other students were likely to recognize the lines, if they had any love for theater and it was a good bet that they did.

The professor called one student after another to the stage. Each performance was brief and Professor Sutton offered criticisms and suggestions on each; both to the actor and the class as a whole.

Some of my fellow students became flustered and messed up horribly so I wasn't much worried about my own performance. Some of the students were rather good, but when Caleb Black took the stage I was transported into the world of William Shakespeare's *A Midsummer Night's Dream*.

Caleb looked out upon his audience and captured us all with his emerald eyes. I knew everyone else felt as I did, as if he was communicating directly with each of us on an individual level. He gazed at us for moment's only, but the room grew completely still. Then, Caleb became Puck, right before our very eyes:

If we shadows have offended,
Think but this, and all is mended,
That you have but slumber'd here
While these visions did appear.
And this weak and idle theme,
No more yielding but a dream,
Gentles, do not reprehend:
If you pardon, we will mend:

And, as I am an honest Puck,
If we have unearned luck
Now to 'scape the serpent's tongue,
We will make amends ere long;
Else the Puck a liar call;
So, good night unto you all.
Give me your hands, if we be friends,
And Robin shall restore amends.

In those brief moments, Caleb not only became Puck he transported us all into another world. It was at that moment that I fell for him. His audience spontaneously applauded, something we had done for no other performer and then Caleb's eyes met my own. We just kept gazing at each other for a few moments. I, for one, was completely smitten by this brilliant young actor. He personified everything I loved about theater.

I don't even remember my own performance. I have no recollection of what I did upon the stage. I remember nothing at all about the rest of the class. All I could think about was Caleb.

After class, I dodged two girls who tried to talk to me, as well as the sexy little blond boy who I'd thought about seducing. He would have to wait until another day. My one thought at the moment was to meet Caleb. I had at last learned his name when Professor Sutton called him to the stage. Caleb. I liked it.

I caught up with Caleb as he was walking down the hallway.

"You're incredible," I said by way of introduction.

He smiled sweetly and even blushed.

"I'm Dorian."

"Caleb."

"Are you busy now, Caleb? I would very much like to take you out to eat."

Caleb seemed a bit overwhelmed by the attention I was giving him.

"I'm...not busy."

"Good, come with me then."

I grasped his elbow and pulled him away with me, all but kidnapping him. We walked from the theater and drama center to the Jordan Avenue Garage where I'd parked my Jag.

"You are incredibly talented," I said.

"I don't know what to say to that, other than 'thank you'."

"You shouldn't be modest. You're going to become a famous actor. I just know it. You are a great actor already."

Caleb blushed.

"I love acting," he said. "It's my escape. When I'm on the stage I'm not me anymore, I'm whomever I wish to be. I'm not just saying lines. I'm living another life."

"Yes! Exactly! That's what I felt when you were in front of the class. You weren't playing the part of Puck, you *were* Puck. I could swear we were in a forest and all was dark. I could feel myself in that place. You didn't need scenery or music to set the mood, you did it all with your expression and your voice."

"It's just something I do," Caleb said. "When I'm on the stage I'm truly not myself anymore. I'm someone else entirely."

"The way you drew us in before you started was amazing. You looked into my eyes for only a moment, but I felt as if you gazed into them forever. I felt as if all you were doing on that stage was just for me and I know everyone else felt the same. You cast a spell over all."

"I like to make contact with an audience when I can. Of course, during most performances it's very difficult to see anyone in the audience. Stage lights are often blinding."

"Have you performed much? My guess is that you have. You are what, eighteen, and yet you have the polish of an actor twice and more your age."

"Yes, I'm eighteen and I've performed a great deal. I was in every stage production at school, starting in grade school. I have been Tom Sawyer, Sweeney Todd, Romeo, the scarecrow in the *Wizard of Oz*, and so many others. I've done a lot of local theater, starting when I was only eight. I've spent every summer in an old theater instead of outside playing sports like all the other kids."

"Were you ever Puck?"

"Not before today."

Caleb grinned and my heart soared. I leaned over and kissed him upon the lips. I didn't hesitate for a second even though we were surrounded by students as we walked along Jordan Avenue.

I extended my hand and Caleb took it in his own. I was ready to burst with happiness.

"This is yours?" Caleb asked, gazing at my Jag convertible. "I don't even have a car."

"I think of it as my toy," I said, laughing. "Climb in."

I drove Caleb the short distance to the east side and parked in front of Bucceto's. I led him inside and soon we were seated at a booth.

"Order anything you like, but everything is delicious here," I said.

"I eat at Burger King a lot. Places like this are too expensive for a poor college boy."

"They aren't for a rich college boy," I said, grinning.

When our waiter came I ordered a spinach artichoke dip appetizer, a shrimp Vera Cruz pasta dinner which came with a salad and garlic bread, and a Coke. Caleb ordered a fettuccine alfredo pasta dinner and a Coke.

"Thank you for bringing me here," Caleb said. "This is very nice."

"It's nice for Bloomington, at least, not that I'm putting down Bloomington. I love it here. I've been here since the beginning of the summer."

"Really? Your parents let you come so early?"

"My parents are dead. I do whatever I want."

"I'm sorry."

"Things happen. I don't dwell on their deaths. They wouldn't want me to do that. Life is for living. That's exactly what they would tell me if they were here."

"I think I'd have difficulty adjusting if my parents died. I can't even imagine it."

"It wasn't easy at first, but...life goes on. I knew I could either wallow in grief or do my best to enjoy my life. If my parent's deaths taught me one thing, it's that you never know when you're time is up. I'm young, but I could be dead by this time tomorrow so I don't have time to waste mourning."

"You do move fast," Caleb said with a grin.

"I suppose you mean the kiss? I go after what I want and what I wanted at that moment was to kiss you."

"That was quite a risk to take. Most guys aren't into kissing other guys, even one as incredibly attractive as you."

"If I hadn't taken the risk, I wouldn't have experienced the kiss. I'd probably be sounding you out right now to figure out if you're into guys or not. Then, I'd have to wait for the right moment to go for it. My way is much simpler, don't you think?"

"Yes, but it takes balls."

"I've got balls," I said, groping myself.

"Why me?" Caleb asked. "I'm sure you can have just about any guy you want and there are much hotter guys on campus."

"You underestimate yourself and your acting talent impressed me. It will give us something to talk about after we have sex."

"You're quite confident."

"Yes, I am, but don't think I mean to take you back to my room and have my way with you after we finish eating. I want more from you than just a hookup and if we start with a hookup that's all it will likely ever be."

"What if I want to hookup now?"

"We don't always get what we want," I said, mischievously.

"You're just a bit evil."

"I'm more than a bit evil, but I want more than what's in your pants, Caleb..."

"Black."

"Caleb Black."

"Hello, Caleb Black. I'm Dorian Gray."

Caleb did not comment on my last name, but raised his right eyebrow ever so slightly. I hadn't thought of the similarity of our names until they were spoken out loud; Black and Gray.

Our food arrived and we talked while we ate. Caleb was also a freshman. He was a theater major and he lived in Teter Quad. We began discussing Broadway shows and I loved the way his eyes lit up as he spoke of the various performances he'd managed to see. I must admit I was completely taken by him.

Despite my words at the table I was tempted to make him back to my suite after supper, but I knew it would be a mistake. Sex I could easily obtain elsewhere. I would have Caleb. I had no doubt of that. When I had him it would not be mere sex, but love-making. Caleb Black was far too fine to treat like a mere trick.

Chapter 4: The Beguiler is Beguiled

Seth

I listened with rapt attention as Dorian talked endlessly about his newfound love. I must admit I was completely jealous. I knew I could never have him, but I adored Dorian and to hear him speak of another with such unbridled enthusiasm was pure torment. Still, I was happy that he was happy and I had never seen him happier.

"You were so right about indulging oneself, Seth. On the day I met Caleb I wanted to kiss him, so I did. We were surrounded by others and I had no idea how he would react, but I took what I wanted and now he is mine. I've been bold in seeking out sex, but this...this is on a whole other scale."

"Indeed it is. I am glad you have come around to my philosophy. Daulton thinks I've been a terrible influence. He fears I've corrupted you."

"What is corrupt about fearlessly going after one's heart's desire? What is corrupt about enjoying life before one is destroyed by death?"

"Daulton fears you will become perverted and depraved."

"Aren't we all perverted and depraved to some degree?" Dorian asked.

"We are all quite perverted. Few of us have the courage to explore our perversions and depravities. I must admit I am surprised your boldness has turned towards love. A young man of your age..."

"Should be fucking everything that moves?"

I laughed.

"If Daulton could hear you now he would be quite sure I have ruined you."

"Nonsense. You merely opened my eyes to reality and I thank you for it. As for sex, I haven't neglected it. I'm far too picky to fuck anything that moves, but I sate my desires at will."

"A young man of your extraordinary beauty should be choosy. After all, why settle for the cheap seats when you can sit down front? I wonder what your new love might think of your sexual escapades."

"What he doesn't know won't hurt me. Besides, I'm doing it for us. I cannot possibly move as slowly as I should with Caleb with my cock constantly throbbing with longing and I do so long for him. I could have him in an instant, of course, but I mean for this to be a romance of theatrical proportions and it cannot be if I treat him like a whore."

"True, and as you have pointed out there are plenty of whores about to sate you lust."

"Exactly, although calling them whores is incorrect as no money changes hands, but just calling them hookups doesn't have the same impact."

"True enough. When was your last hookup, Dorian?"

"I believe you are a dirty old man, or rather dirty older man because you are not yet old."

"All correct."

"My last hookup was just before coming here. It was quite spontaneous."

"Spontaneous pleasures are always the best," I commented.

"I strolled through the HPER on the way back from the library. I had a sudden urge so I checked out a restroom on the lower level that is said to be cruisey."

"I take it that it was."

"Mmm, yes. I was not there thirty seconds when a young man near my age entered and eyed me. I had never done such a thing before so I didn't know the rules, but I motioned toward a stall with my head. He followed me in, closed the door, and was on his knees in a second."

"Was he good?"

"He was very, very good. I exploded in his mouth in under five minutes. I could have held off, but I didn't want to be late in meeting you and my only real goal was to get off."

"Never worry about being late for an appointment with me if there is pleasure to be obtained in doing so, as long as I get all the details."

I grinned.

"He gave me his number. I kept it, but I don't know if I'll use it or not. It's so very easy to find willing guys on campus."

"For you, at least. I'm sure plenty of girls throw themselves at your feet as well."

"Several girls have shown interest in me already, but I do not encourage them. I do not wish to be cruel and I have no interest in them, no sexual interest, that is."

Dorian talked on at length about Caleb. It was quite clear Dorian was infatuated with him, obsessed even. Dorian possessed the power to charm anyone and yet the charmer had been charmed. I could see no happy ending in it, but there were no happy endings in life. All life ends in death and the only thing that matters is what happens before the end. Dorian was setting himself up for disappointment and pain but the pleasures of being in love are many. He was very young and he needed to be burned by the fire so he would know not to touch it again.

I smiled as I listened to my creation speak, for he was my creation. Dorian Gray was not the same boy I met only a few weeks before in Daulton's studio. He was changed and I had changed him with the introduction of a simple and powerful idea. Daulton believed I corrupted him, but I merely revealed a truth. Dorian was young and beautiful. The world was his, but only while his youth and beauty lasted. When it was gone the world would turn its back on him.

I was never so beautiful as Dorian, but of course I was once as young. I possessed the beauty that all youth possesses, but it had forsaken me. I had been wise enough to take what advantage I could before my youth faded. Now, I found other delights that did not so much require beauty. One of those delights was the company of handsome young men and Dorian was the most attractive of them all. If youths were works of art, Dorian was a masterpiece. He was a Da Vinci, a Michelangelo, a Renoir, a Monet. His every movement was fluid grace. His every word a melody. Thanks to me, he could see himself as I and countless others saw him. I had done him a tremendous service by telling him the value of his youth and beauty. He would not now easily squander it. He would not grow old before he realized the value of what he possessed. He would appreciate and use his beauty in the brief space of time that was allotted to him.

"What are you smiling about, Seth? You look quite pleased with yourself."

"I am happy that you are happy. I am pleased because you took my compliments and advice to heart and did not turn aside from them as others have done."

"I think I would have turned aside the compliments if it hadn't been for the portrait. I had never really looked at myself before. Perhaps it would be more accurate to say I'd never truly *seen* myself. As for your advice, it is entirely sound and will no doubt save me many regrets."

Dorian walked over to me, grasped my chin, and kissed me briefly on the lips.

"Thank you, Seth."

Dorian smiled at me and then left me. I watched him as he departed. He left me with a longing to be young again. It was a longing that was not a stranger to me. I had spent my youth well, but Dorian...Dorian had the opportunity to be a god.

Chapter Five: Dorian Seduces a Straight Wrestler

I stood gazing at my portrait. The beautiful young man gazed back at me. He mocked me. He would forever stay as beautiful and young as he was on the day the painting was finished. I had already aged. A few short weeks was far too short of time for any noticeable change, but that didn't mean change was not taking place. I would look much the same six months from now, changed and yet not changed enough to perceive. How long before there was a visible difference? Two years? Three? I was eighteen. In three years I would be twenty-one. In ten years more I would be thirty-one. By then the wrinkles would begin to appear and once they did they would only become more pronounced. My hair would begin to thin and eventually I'd have a bald spot. The young man in the portrait smiled at me, mocking me. He knew he would remain forever beautiful while I would not. I hated him for it. I wished again in my heart what I had said out loud in Daulton's studio all those weeks ago, that my portrait could age and I could remain forever young! Seth was right. Nothing had value except youth and beauty and I would have given my soul to keep the pair forever.

I left the painting to itself and walked into the living room. I picked up one of my texts for my acting class and began to read. Already there were assignments and the reading required was considerable. I intended to get a few chapters out of the way, then perhaps go in search of some distraction before bed.

The sound of running footsteps and yelling outside in the hallway derailed my train of thought. I liked to be in the thick of things on campus, but I preferred some quiet for reading, at least when I wanted to concentrate. I walked over to the stereo and put on some Vivaldi. I was more into rock than classical, but classical made for a good background noise that would disguise the ruckus outside and not distract me. Had it not been growing dark, I might have taken my books to Dunn's Woods or some other quiet campus location to read, but the light outside was failing fast.

I sat back down in my chair and began to read again. The excitement of the university called out to me. My new philosophy of life demanded that I have fun. I had to balance that with other things I wanted and one of those things was to experience the world of theater to the fullest. At the moment, that meant studying. It was not as fun as a party, or sex, or having guys and girls flirt with me, but it was important to me and I was strong enough to follow through.

I found that I enjoyed the required reading for my acting class. The world of theater enthralled me and so even the smallest details interested me. I was less enthused about the assignments for my morning classes, but I still derived a certain pleasure from the mere fact I was a college boy. I was even giving thought to staying at IU for graduate studies, although that was rather premature seeing as this was only the beginning of my freshman year!

At ten, I left my books behind and walked outside. There were students walking around and cars passing on Third Street and Jordan Avenue, but it was fairly quiet. I just stood in front of Read for a while breathing in the summer air.

"Freshman?"

I looked down, a couple of girls I did not know had approached while I was trying to gaze at the stars.

"Yeah."

"Us too. If you're not doing anything tonight, there's a party going on in the Varsity Villas up by the stadium—music, alcohol, and just everyone getting to know each other. You should come."

The girl speaking to me was blond and rather attractive. If I had been into girls I would have gone after her in a flash. Her friend, who had dark hair, wasn't hard on the eyes either.

"I might drop by, I don't know. I've definitely had enough studying for my first night."

"Well, we hope to see you there. If you need a ride..."

"I'm good."

The girls were disappointed that I didn't volunteer to jump in a car with them, but if I encouraged them it would be all the harder to rid myself of them later. If I was going to a party I didn't want to be shackled to girls.

A party was an excellent idea so I walked to my Jag and headed for the Villas. As a freshman, I was supposed to keep my car parked off campus or by the stadium, but there were ways around that for those with cash. I didn't know if I could have handled not having immediate access to my car.

There were apartments everywhere up by the stadium. It was the party area of IU. I'd already attended one party at the Varsity Villas before the semester started, so I knew where I was going. I drove up Jordan Avenue until I hit 17th Street. I took a left, then after passing Assembly Hall and the Memorial Stadium, turned right on Dunn Street. I didn't have an exact address for the party, but I knew it would not be difficult to locate.

The Villas were expansive and almost a little village onto themselves. I parked when I came to a mass of cars and then followed the loud music to its source.

Paper cups, beer cans, and liquor bottles littered the lawn where a throng of college students milled about and drank. A cup was pressed into my hand by a drunk boy before I even got near. I had no trouble obtaining alcohol at parties. Someone was always willing to hook me up.

I didn't see the girls who had invited me, which was something of a relief. I could already tell that girls were going to be a huge problem. It was going to be difficult to keep them at bay. I had no intention of keeping my sexual orientation a secret and the more girls who saw me locking lips with another guy the fewer there would be to annoy me. Being gay was not that big of a deal at IU and anyone who had a problem with it could go fuck themselves.

I mingled, chatting with whoever came in range, flirting with the hottest guys, and ditching girls as fast as possible. I eyed a slightly inebriated hunk with dark brown, straight hair and a killer body. The boy was a little older than me I guessed and built. I noticed him looking at me and then looking away when I turned my gaze in his direction. It was a sure sign that he wasn't entirely comfortable with the thoughts running through his head. That most likely meant he was hot for me, wasn't gay, and either had no experience with guys or felt guilty about whatever experiences he had indulged in. I had learned to read guys like him during my high school years, but back then I didn't have the balls to make a move. Now, I did.

I closed in on the hunk and chatted him up. I learned he was a junior and a varsity wrestler for IU. I could easily believe it with his powerful muscles and sculpted body. Just looking at him made my cock throb.

Josh, that was his name, kept gazing at me with hunger, but didn't make a move.

I talked about my interest in theater which was an intentional tip off I was gay. Josh talked about wrestling and I kept picturing his singlet, skin-tight, against his powerful pecs, and hot ass. I decided then I was going to have him.

"Let's blow this party," I said. "We can go somewhere quieter to talk."

Josh chugged his beer and crushed the cup. He followed me away from the music and the crowd.

"Damn! Nice car!"

"Thanks," I said.

"You must be rich or have rich parents to have a car like this. I'm stuck with a shit worn-out Chevy Nova."

"I'm rich," I said bluntly. "Get in."

I didn't ask where Josh wanted to go. I drove him straight back to Read. He didn't resist as I led him inside and up to my suite.

"Where are your roommates?"

"I don't have any," I said.

"Wow, must be nice. I share an apartment two nerds. Those dudes will *never* get laid."

"I'm sure that's not a problem for you," I said.

"Nope, the girls love my bod."

Josh swayed slightly. He was drunk. He was also incredibly hot. I closed in on him and gazed into his eyes. He looked slightly uncomfortable, but he didn't pull away. I leaned in and he put his hand on my chest.

"I don't kiss, man. I'm straight."

"Tomorrow, yes, but not tonight."

Josh could have easily restrained me, but I pulled him close and pressed my lips to his. I kissed him deeply. At first, he didn't kiss back, but soon he responded and our tongues entwined. He pressed his crotch into me and moaned into my mouth.

I pulled his tank-top over his head. Damn! Josh was built, even more so than I'd guessed. I ran my hands over his pecs and his six-pack as we continued to make out. I ran my hands lower and groped him. He moaned even louder.

Josh pulled my shirt over my head and ran his hands over my chest. He kneaded my butt-cheeks as he pressed himself into me. I knew what he was thinking, but it wasn't going to happen. I intended to have him, not the other way around.

I worked Josh into a sexy frenzy. I stripped him naked and shed the rest of my clothes. I had him moaning and panting. I pushed him toward and then down onto the couch. I pulled his legs up.

"No. I don't take it in the ass, man."

"For me you do. You know you want it. You know you want me inside you. No one will ever know."

Josh feebly struggled as I grabbed his legs and pulled him toward me so that his back was on the couch and his hot ass hanging off the edge. He put up a token resistance.

"No, man. I can't. I've never..."

"You know you're curious about it. If you don't like it I'll stop. This is your chance, man. We're alone, no one will disturb us, and no one will ever know."

"I am sooo drunk," Josh said and laughed.

I took that as permission to continue. I needed his permission because he was probably five-times stronger than me.

I positioned myself and ever so slowly slid inside him. He grunted and a wave of pain passed over his handsome face. I held still for a few moments. I had to be careful not to hurt him too much or this party would be over fast.

I took my time and soon enough, I was inside him. I began to slowly thrust and Josh began to moan.

I began to go at it harder and faster. Something instinctive took over and nothing mattered but getting as deep inside him as possible. I abandoned all pretense of taking it easy and Josh submitted to me.

In too short a time I moaned and experienced an intense orgasm. Josh finished himself off and was soon dressing and looking anywhere in the room but at me.

"You won't tell anyone, right? I have a girlfriend and..."

"It never happened," I said.

Josh beat it out of my suite quickly. I grinned as I closed and locked the door. I experienced the heady rush of seducing a straight-boy. I hoped I crossed Josh's path on campus. It would be worth much to look him in the eyes and see the expression on his face.

I showered and turned in. If the rest of my days were like this one I was going to love college life.

***

I awakened the next morning, wondering what would go through Josh's mind on this day after. He might try to deny to himself that it had ever happened, but his sore ass would make that all but impossible. Likely, he'd fall back on the "I was drunk" excuse used by all guys who couldn't deal with the fact they liked dick.

Finding parking spots in Bloomington and on campus in particular was an ordeal, so I opted to walk to my classes instead. College wasn't like high school. I didn't have to make it from one class to the next in ten minutes. While on Mondays, Wednesdays, and Fridays I had two morning classes almost back-to-back, I had at least forty-five minutes between all my Tuesday and Thursday courses. I looked for Caleb in my morning classes, but didn't spot him in either. We were both freshman, but IU was a huge school so the chances of us sharing classes was slim.

I had an hour and a half for lunch. I thought about heading downtown, but decided to eat in the Market in the Memorial Union and have a leisurely lunch instead. The Market was kind of like a café, but featured separate little areas with items from Pizza Hut, The Sub Connection, The Charleston Market, which had hot sandwiches, and more. I was surprised to find Chicken Cordon Bleu at The Charleston Market. I filled a cup with Coke at the soda fountain and paid for my purchases.

I had just sat down when two girls walked toward me.

"Mind if we join you?"

"Why not?" I said.

The truth was, I didn't mind a little company. I liked being around others, even if they were girls. I had class in a hour, so I had a built-in method for ditching them.

"I'm Jen and this is Janet."

"Dorian."

"That's an unusual name."

"I guess my parents were original. At least I didn't end up with a boring name."

I looked at what the girls had bought for lunch.

"Why is it that girls always eat healthy and watch their weight?" I asked.

"Other girls maybe, but not us," Janet said. "You merely caught us in a salad mood."

"Yes, it's far easier to catch us in a chocolate or ice cream mood. Our salad moods keep us from getting fat."

"I never think about what I eat. I just eat what I want."

"You have a death wish, don't you?" Janet asked.

"What?"

"Look at you," Jen said. "I bet you don't have an ounce of fat on you and you don't even have to try."

I shrugged.

A really cute boy sat down just a few tables away and I temporarily forgot all about Jen and Janet. They noticed me staring.

"I think we've zeroed in on another one," Jen said to Janet.

"Huh?" I asked, looking back to the girls. Jen smiled.

"He's cute, isn't he?" she asked.

I grinned.

"Very and yes, I am gay."

"What is wrong with us?" Janet asked. "We keep picking out the gay ones."

"Maybe we're all gay," I said, with a mischievous grin.

"That is not even funny," Jen said.

"Maybe not, but perhaps it is true. I had a *straight* boy last night," I said, making quotation marks in the air with my fingers. "I picked him up at a party. He said he had a girlfriend and claimed to be straight, but he still let me fuck him. Hmm, maybe I should keep a record of all the straight boys I hook up with."

"Now you're making me feel like there really aren't any straight boys left."

"I'll leave a few for you. I only like the very hot ones," I said. "The hottest guys are gay, anyway."

"That's true so far. We're two for two. We spotted a hottie yesterday only to find out he was gay, and now here you are. Hot and gay, too."

"I'd say I'm sorry, but it would be a lie. Besides, look at it from my point of view. Girls are always hitting on me and it gets to be a pain in the ass."

"Poor baby," Janet said. "It must be hard to be so very attractive."

I shot her a smirk.

"I enjoy being attractive, I just don't like all the attention that comes with it. Some girls won't take a hint. I have to flat out tell them I'm not interested."

Jen and Janet exchanged a look. I could tell they didn't like me very much. I didn't care. If they didn't like me they wouldn't bother me. Eating lunch with them once was okay, but anything more...

"So tell me about this other hot gay boy you met," I said

"Oh no," Jen said. "He has a boyfriend and I'm not giving you the opportunity to ruin things between them."

"You think I would do that?"

"Yes."

"You're right. I would."

"At least you're honest."

"I have no reason to be otherwise. I don't pretend to be something I'm not for anyone."

"What are you studying?" Jen asked.

It was an obvious attempt to change the topic, but I didn't mind. If we kept going we'd likely end up arguing and I just wanted to have a nice lunch. We talked about our courses for the rest of lunch and then went our separate ways. Jen and Janet seemed like nice girls, but I had no interest in them. I'd probably never seen them again and I had the feeling that was fine with not only me, but them also.

My next class was Ancient Greek Culture 101 which I was taking both to gain some required arts and humanities credits and because I'd always been interested in ancient Greece. I forgot all about the course when I spotted Caleb sitting down near the front. I dropped into the seat beside him and he smiled.

I felt my heart beating faster. I couldn't believe I had met a boy who was so talented and so very attractive. Usually, one or the other was obtainable, but both together was rare. Caleb had a true talent for acting. I had no doubt whatsoever he was going to be famous.

"What did you think about that reading assignment?" he asked.

"Too long, but I enjoyed it. I love anything connected with theater."

"Me too. It's my life!"

"I read it all and then went to a party," I said.

"Yeah? Have a good time?"

"I had a great time. I always do."

I didn't mention fucking the wrestler. I sensed I was going to have to play nice with Caleb. He might not approve my sexual activities. If he were anyone else I wouldn't care, but I had dreams of a future with Caleb.

The class started and we couldn't talk, but I loved just sitting there beside him. I was so glad we had this second class together. It meant I could see him every day of the week.

We both had some spare time before our next classes so we hung out and talked about Broadway shows, Sondheim, and our favorite plays. I was so lost in conversation with Caleb that I wasn't even aware of all the other college students milling around us. When I was with Caleb we were alone, even when we were in a crowd.

I walked Caleb to his class. I could tell he was pleased that I paid so much attention to him. I yearned to lean in and kiss him, but I decided to wait just a little longer. I liked to sexually torment myself sometimes and I also wanted to play my cards just right with Caleb. He wasn't a hookup that I could use and discard, like the boy the night before. I had to watch my step.

I walked to Dunn's Woods after dropping off Caleb and did some reading for my Ancient Greek Culture class. I had some time to kill, but not enough time to really do anything like go shopping or cruise for boys so I figured I might as well get some schoolwork out of my way. I sat on a stone bench in front of the Rose Well House and read about the Greeks until I figured it was time to head to my next class.

I walked around campus, turning more than a few heads. One girl actually walked into one of her friends because she was so busy gawking at me. I grinned as I walked on. Girls could be entertaining if I didn't let them get too close. As long as I kept moving, I was safe. Once Caleb and I became an item we'd be together a lot. That would help keep the girls at bay.

***

The rest of the day was a whirlwind of activity. I had so many opening assignments from my classes that I had to return to my suite right after my last class and hit the books. College would have been much more fun if I didn't have to attend classes. Actually, what would have been the most fun was taking only theater related classes. I wished I had the time to take them all, but that was an impossibility. It's too bad I was stuck with course requirements that had little or nothing to do with theater. I enjoyed my Ancient Greek Culture class, but some of the others...not so much.

I took the time to walk over to Mother Bear's pizza and have supper. I ordered myself a Divine Swine pizza which was topped with pepperoni, sausage, ham, and bacon. While I waited, I read the graffiti written all over the table and the wooden booth. I gazed around the room. It was everywhere.

It was relaxing to get away from my books. I felt like I was turning into some kind of book worm and that didn't appeal to me in the least. Of course, I didn't have to attend college at all. The point of school for most was to get a good job and make money. I already had more money than I could spend and more came in every day. I didn't need school, that was for sure, but college allowed me to study drama and that's what I wanted. I could spend my life doing anything I pleased and I pleased to immerse myself in the world of theater. Everything had a price and the price tag attached to the life I wanted included school. Besides, my non-theater courses weren't that bad. Some I even enjoyed.

I picked up a copy of the IDS, the *Indiana Daily Student*, while I was waiting on my pizza. I browsed through the pages and sipped my Coke until I came to a photo that caught my eye.

"So he's a football player," I said out loud.

I read the caption under a photo taken at a recent football practice. It read, "Freshman Brendan Brewer gets his first taste of Indiana football." I looked at the accompanying article, but it said nothing about Brendan. It was all about the team's chances for this season and the returning quarterback, Gabrial Diaddio. At least I now had a name to put with that handsome face and gorgeous body. I decided then and there to attend the first football game of the season. With any luck maybe I'd catch up with Brendan Brewer. When I did, I intended to have him.

My pizza arrived. Mother Bear's lived up to its reputation. It truly did have the best pizza around. That and it's location just across Third Street from Read made it my new favorite place.

I sat there eating and thinking about Brendan Brewer. I mentally undressed him in my mind. He had to have one gorgeous body hidden under that uniform. I had half a mind to head to Forest Quad and stake it out after supper, but I might sit there for hours and never see him. It wasn't as if there was just one exit either. He could slip out one while I was watching another. No, a football game was my best bet. At the very least, I'd get to see him play. At the best, I could corner him after the game. I grinned. IU became increasingly more fun with each passing day.

Chapter Six: The Effortless Seduction of Weston Mayfair

I walked into my Acting for Majors class the next afternoon and there sat Caleb Black, looking as sexy as ever. Was it only 48 hours since I'd fallen in love with him? Was it love? It was obsession at least. I hadn't been able to get him out of my mind. Even when I was plowing that straight wrestler I was thinking of Caleb, his sexy body, and his golden voice. I wondered if he'd be a star of stage or screen? Perhaps both. Talent like his came once in a generation.

We did some acting exercises in class that once more proved Caleb's superiority. There was some talent in class, but he was a star. I could not wait to see him perform an entire play. He would be the lead, surely! If not, it would be a crime.

Acting class was over before it even began. At least it seemed that way to me. Was it because Caleb was near, because I was bewitched by his performance, or both?

This time, I did not have to seek him out after class. He lingered. We tossed our backpacks over our shoulders and navigated our way to the wooded paths to the side of the auditorium. Some paths were paved and others gravel, they wandered beside and over the Jordan River.

"Do you know why this is called the Jordan River? It's only a stream, truly," I asked my handsome companion.

"I think it's real name is Spanker's Branch. I heard that somewhere, but everyone calls it the Jordan River. I have no idea why."

"I suppose it is one of the strange mysteries of IU."

"There are others?" Caleb asked as we walked aimlessly.

"Well, my dorm is supposedly haunted by a girl in the yellow dress. She had beautiful long black hair. She dated a young med student, but they had a violent argument and he killed her."

"Some boyfriend."

"No kidding. She is supposed to cause electrical problems and such, stereos and what-have-you turning on or off by themselves. She's been seen by some residents in previous years. I've never seen her and my electrical appliances work just fine, but I haven't lived in Read long. Perhaps I'll run across her yet."

Caleb laughed.

"There is more to her story, but I've just heard bits and pieces. There are stories of ghosts in different parts of IU. This place has been here a long time."

"No kidding."

We walked past the Memorial Union and into Dunn Meadow before turning left. We wandered among the paths until we came to what is known as the Old Crescent, where the oldest buildings of IU are located. I led Caleb into Dunn's Woods and there we walked among the wooded pathways.

There was still so much I didn't know about Caleb. How could I? He filled my thoughts to such an extent I felt like I'd known him for years, but it had been only hours since we met. It didn't matter. I knew all I needed to already.

I stopped and turned to Caleb. I gazed into his eyes for a moment and then leaned in and kissed him. He kissed me back hungrily. I wanted to rip off his clothes and ravish him, but there were other students around. That's the very reason I had not taken him back to my suite. I knew that if we were alone, I would not be able to stop myself once I kissed him. I did not want to go too far too fast with Caleb. Ours was to be a great romance and all would be ruined if we reduced it to sex. I would have him, certainly, but only at the proper time. Our love scene would come well into the play.

Caleb smiled at me. I took his hand and we wandered among the trees in silence, just enjoying each other's company. We passed other couples holding hands, although they were all male/female couples. Caleb and I made the handsomest couple of all. The others could only hope to be us.

Several students saw us together holding hands. I wanted them to see. I wanted everyone to know that Caleb was mine.

"Where would you like to eat? I'll take you anywhere," I said.

"Dorian, I don't want you spending money on me. You took me out once already..."

"Shh. I have more money than I can ever spend and I want to spend some of it on you. Name it. I will take you anywhere you wish. Please. It will make me happy."

Caleb grinned and shook his head.

"I'm not much one for fancy restaurants," Caleb said.

"Good, because there aren't any in Bloomington, not by the standards of New York or London at least. There are plenty that are wonderful here regardless, so choose."

"Opie Taylors."

"Then Opie Taylors it is."

While it seemed as if we were deep in a forest, Dunn's Woods was located on the very western edge of IU. In only a couple of minutes Caleb and I were walking down Kirkwood, one of the busiest streets in all of Bloomington. Here were located bars like Kilroys and Nick's English Hut, shops galore, restaurants, the public library, banks, and more. We walked up to the square and turned right on North College Avenue.

Soon, we were seated in a booth in Opie Taylors. It wasn't fancy in the least, but I liked the large booths. The backs of the benches were high and there was what amounted to a roof overhead. It was as if we were sitting in our own little cottage. TVs played sporting events while families and college students ate.

"I hear the burgers here are great," Caleb said.

I took Caleb's advice and ordered a Buffalo Bleu Cheese Burger when our waitress arrived. Caleb ordered a Cajun Burger.

I sat back and smiled at Caleb as the waitress returned with our Cokes.

"What are you grinning about?"

"You. I am so glad we met and that you didn't object when I slid my tongue in your mouth."

Caleb smiled back.

"Most of the girls on campus and probably half the guys would beg you to stick your tongue in their mouth."

"The girls are a bit of a problem here," I said.

"Having trouble keeping them away?"

"Yes."

"You have interesting problems, Dorian."

"I know it doesn't sound like a problem and there are frat boys who would smack me for complaining about such a thing but it's very annoying when girls hit on me everywhere I go. I feel like wearing a sign that says, 'Unless you're a hot guy, I'm not interested'."

"Now that would be an interesting sight. Did you hold my hand for so long on campus to keep the girls away?"

"Only partly. Mostly, I held it because I want everyone to know how much you mean to me and I simply wanted to hold your hand."

"You are too good to be true, Dorian Gray."

"Oh, I'm not perfect. Close, but not quite."

Caleb threw a napkin at me.

"I'm so excited about our assignment. Have you chosen a part yet?" Caleb asked.

"No."

"Auditions are Friday."

"Yes, but we've only just left class." I laughed.

"This will be great experience. I've auditioned for plays before, of course, but I know it will be different in college."

"It's a unique idea. Casting the entire play out of each class and then choosing the best in each for the fall production."

"Yes. We'll be competing against four other classes. That means I'll have to beat out four other J. Pierrepont Finch's *if* I land the role in our class."

"I'm glad you are going to audition for the lead. I was going to suggest it," I said.

"Yeah?"

"How could you not? *How to Succeed in Business Without Really Trying* has already been a top show on Broadway twice and you just know it will be again. A musical comedy will be a great way to showcase your talents and get you noticed here at IU."

"How do you know about my talents?"

"I knew you were going to be a great actor the first day of class. As soon as you got up in front of the class I was mesmerized. You completely transported me out of that room. When you stopped I was disoriented because I couldn't figure out why I was sitting in a classroom."

Caleb just sat there speechless. He looked as if he might cry.

"That's the nicest thing anyone had ever said to me," Caleb said.

"You'll be hearing much nicer things from others soon. I know it."

"Wow, you take my breath away, Dorian."

"Kiss me."

Caleb leaned across the table and we shared a kiss. Some heads turned our way, but what did we care? We *were* drama students and our very lives were a performance. I had planned from the beginning for our romance to be theatrical and what was theater without an audience?

Our burgers arrived and they were delicious. I liked fine things. Opie Taylors was not fancy, but the burgers were indeed fine. The more time I spent with Caleb, the more I knew I had chosen my companion well.

After we had eaten, I took Caleb to a little chocolate shop I'd spotted just south of the other side of the square. There, I bought us the most delicious turtles which we shared as dessert. I led Caleb up the street and into a flower shop where I bought him a dozen long-stemmed roses.

"Dorian, I...I don't know what to say. No one has ever made such a fuss over me."

"This is only the beginning," I said with a smile.

"Dorian, you really shouldn't spend..."

"Shh," I said, placing my finger on his lips. "Money is nothing to me. You are everything."

"I still feel guilty."

"Don't. My parents left me a fortune and they left me investments which constantly make more money. While I was buying you these roses I was making more than I was spending."

"Are you so very rich?"

"Let's just say that I wish I had a dime for every dime I have." I grinned. "The point is don't feel guilty. It makes me happy to spend money on you. I've spent it to make myself happy and now, at last, I have someone I care deeply about to spend it on too."

"Oh, Dorian. You are too much."

Caleb hugged me. His tight body pressed against mine filled me with love and lust. Yes, we would be worthy of a Broadway play ourselves.

We walked back toward campus. I could have spent hours more with Caleb, but he was eager to study his script in preparation for his audition. I needed to give some thought as to what part I would try for as well, and then there was more schoolwork...it never ended.

I walked Caleb back to his dorm, Teter Quad, which was on the south side of 10th Street and not far west of Read. It was a relatively short walk and all too soon it was time to say goodbye.

Caleb hugged me, then kissed me.

"I'll see you in class tomorrow. I'm swamped with homework and this audition, but maybe we can do something after class on Friday?" Caleb asked.

"It's a date."

"Thank you for the flowers and for...everything."

I leaned in and kissed him again, then reluctantly parted.

I walked away from Teter Quad and back toward Read. I felt as if I could fly. I wanted to rush to Seth and tell him everything. I was bursting to share my feelings with someone, but I had to think rationally. I had much schoolwork and I needed to plan for my own audition. I intended to try for a minor role, but I wanted to do the best job possible because Caleb would be watching. There was no way I could match his level of talent, but I had to be the best I could be.

I pulled out the script when I made it back to Read. I wasn't sure about singing. Oh, I could sing and sing well, but I'd rather act or...the book narrator. I had a great voice and I could project. Yes, that just might be the part for me.

I let the matter rest while I dove into other schoolwork, but not before making myself some cappuccino. A cappuccino machine really should have been standard in every dorm room.

Mine had already helped me stay up late studying and the semester has just began. I almost couldn't believe most students drank mere coffee.

I sat at the table with my cappuccino and began my work. There was something satisfying about studying and completing minor tasks. College gave me something I didn't even know I needed, structure. I loved college life more with each passing day.

I kept at my work for more than three hours. I sat back and stretched. I needed to get out of my suite for a while and I still had a decision to make.

I left Read, headed across Jordan Avenue and walked aimlessly through campus. My destination didn't matter. I needed to pick a part for my audition. I'd considered the narrator, but I had decided that didn't really appeal to me. J.B. Biggley, the boss? No, that was far too large a part. I wanted something small. Part of me would have been happy to work only behind the scenes, but I did want to experience what it was like to act in a real play, even if the audience was only my classmates. I did intend to take the audition seriously. I wanted to experience the world of theater and no true actor would make a half-ass attempt to get a part. I wanted a part in the fall production, just not a large part. My chances of landing a small part were much better than my chances of walking away with a lead. I would leave the leads to the truly talented, like Caleb.

I looked up. I'd already walked to Ballentine Hall without realizing it. I gazed around. The campus looked different at night, but still possessed a quiet beauty. It was like one big park. I walked across the street to Beck Chapel and stopped to gaze at the little graveyard the lay beside it. Some of the tombstones looked very old.

Bub Frump, the snobbish nephew? No. That part was also too large and I doubted I could get into it. Mr. Bratt, the personnel manager? No. That was still too large a part. Hmm.

I started walking again. I walked up the side of the Memorial Union and entered through the entrance by the circular drive. I climbed the stairs and walked around the student union aimlessly.

Mr. Twimble, the head of the mailroom? I stopped for a moment. Perhaps. He had a few lines, enough to be significant, but not that many. He appeared early in the play, but then disappeared. He did have a song with J. Pierrepont Finch, but if I remembered correctly, in the film version the song was short and Mr. Twimble's parts were almost spoken rather than sung. I could handle that. Yes, Mr. Twimble it would be. If Caleb landed the lead, and there was little doubt about that in my mind, we would be on the stage together. I was far too young for the part, but then the entire cast would be too young for all the parts. It didn't matter. We were actors after all.

I found myself in one of the lounges. Five different students were splayed out on different chairs and couches, asleep. A couple of others were quietly reading. I sat down in front of the fireplace, stretched out my legs and gazed at the flames.

I grew a bit drowsy sitting there. I was comfortable and cozy. I could have nodded off and joined the other sleeping students, but I remained awake.

"Hey."

I looked up.

"I don't mean to disturb you, but you're in my acting class, right?"

It was the cute blond boy from class.

"Yes, I'm Dorian."

"I'm Weston."

"Have a seat," I said.

I remembered Weston well from class. He was quite small, probably about 5'5" and I doubted he weighed over a hundred pounds. He was very slim and boyishly handsome.

"I meant to talk to you after class, but I haven't had the chance. You're usually with Caleb."

There was an implied question in Weston's tone which asked *Are Caleb and you an item?* I smiled. The boy was hot for me. He was cute, even if he was small.

"How old are you?" I asked.

"You think I'm too young to be in college, don't you? Most people do. I'm eighteen. I know I look younger. I've had three different girls ask if was lost when I was walking around campus."

"You're quite talented," I said. "I've noticed you in class."

"I have a long way to go, but thanks. I wish I was half the actor Caleb is. Isn't he incredible?"

"Oh yes. Someday, we'll both be telling people we went to school with him. He's going to be big."

"He's also really attractive, although not as attractive as you." Weston blushed and it made him especially cute.

Weston gazed at me. I could read both the fear and desire in his eyes. I leaned in and kissed him. He closed his eyes and kissed me back. We broke our kiss. Weston smiled at me and then I kissed him again, more deeply this time. We sat there on the couch and made out before the dancing flames in the fireplace. I was becoming increasingly aroused.

"Let's go back to my place," I said.

I stood grasped Weston by the hand and pulled him to his feet. We walked side-by-side out of the Memorial Union and toward Read. I took the shortest route possible this time. My dick was straining against my shorts. I couldn't wait to get Weston naked and I knew he was chomping at the bit.

We were on each other the moment I closed the door to my suite. Our clothes went flying and our hands and lips were everywhere at once. Weston looked much more his age with his clothes off. He was short and slim, but muscled and defined. He was definitely no boy. I pushed down on his shoulders and he didn't resist. He went to work and I moaned.

I only let him stay on his knees a few minutes. As much as I wanted to relieve the pressure in my groin I also wanted to savor it, and I had other plans for Weston.

I pulled Weston to his feet. We necked some more and traveled up and down each other's body. When I had him panting and moaning I led him into my bedroom. I pushed him down on the bed and climbed on top of him. I made out with him some more, running my hands and then tongue over his smooth, firm body.

I stood, opened the nightstand drawer, and pulled out a condom. Weston eyed me nervously as I tore open the package.

"I've um...I've never..."

"I'll go easy at first and I'll use lots of lube. It will hurt a little but then it will feel so incredible you'll want it again and again and again."

Weston gazed at me with lust-glazed eyes. Arousal was a far more useful tool for getting what one wanted from a male than alcohol. It was every man's Kryptonite.

I guided Weston onto his stomach and gave him a pillow for his head. I made generous use of the lube. I put my legs on either sides of Weston and lowered myself upon him. I positioned myself against him and gently pushed. He was tight, but I kept trying, slowly but persistently. I slipped in just a bit and Weston hissed in pain.

"Take it easy. This is the worst part. Once I'm in you'll like it. I promise."

I went slowly, but pushed myself deeper into Weston. He cried out and gripped the pillow in his fists. I stopped before I was all the way in. Weston was breathing hard and whimpering.

"Relax. This is where it starts to feel good. Next time, it will be easier and if you do it now and then it won't hurt at all."

I pulled out slightly and pushed in again. I was very gentle at first. It was hard to hold back when I wanted to sink myself into him as deeply as possible, but I was patient. I'd have what I wanted, just not quite yet.

Weston began to relax. His breathing calmed and he began to moan a little. I went faster and deeper. He moaned more. His moans were high pitched, but satisfying. Soon, I was able to sink myself into him all the way.

From that point on I was able to go faster and harder. Weston moaned, whimpered, and cried out. I knew he was experiencing a mixture of pleasure and pain. He was likely on the verge of asking me to stop, and yet didn't want me to stop. I wasn't sure I'd stop if he asked.

I was consumed with our coupling. Nothing mattered but going as deep and fast as I could. I flipped Weston onto his back, pulled his legs over my shoulders, and took him again. I stared into his eyes as I used him.

I was beginning to perspire. I moaned and groaned. I'd made it last as long as I could but I couldn't hold back anymore. I thrust harder and harder, then moaned as my orgasm spread throughout my body. Weston experienced his orgasm at nearly the same time. Neither of us had touched him even once, but he exploded all over his own torso.

I rolled off him, panting, and we lay there side-by-side for a few moments catching our breath.

"You were right. It hurt at first. I didn't think I could stand it, but once you got going I didn't want you to stop."

"Use the shower to clean up," I said, nodding to the bathroom. "It's late. Want to spend the night?"

"I'd like that." Weston smiled.

I grabbed a washcloth and cleaned off at the sink while Weston showered. When he came out, I was already in bed. He climbed in and lay close beside me. I wrapped my arm around him and we were soon both fast asleep.

When I awakened the next morning Weston was still sleeping. I climbed out of bed, took a shower, and dressed. He stirred as I was putting on my socks.

"Good morning," he said, stretching. He was a sexy little guy.

"Good morning."

Weston climbed out of bed and retrieved his clothes from the floor. The sight of his hot little ass aroused me and I savored the feeling. Last night, Weston's ass had been mine and it would be again.

"Coffee?" I asked.

"I don't want to be any trouble."

"You aren't and we need to talk."

Weston nodded.

I walked into the kitchen area and put on some French roast. My gourmet coffee maker was extra-fast. By the time Weston came out of the bedroom it was nearly finished. I pulled mugs out of the cabinet, poured us each a cup, and walked to the table. We sat down.

"About last night," I said. "What happened needs to remain between us. I don't care who knows I'm gay, but I like to keep my private life private."

"Okay. I can understand that. It will be hard not telling anyone because you're so incredibly hot, but...I won't."

"Good, because if you tell anyone it will never happen again."

"Does that mean it will happen again if I keep my mouth shut?" Weston asked hopefully.

"Yes, if I'm in the mood and I'm always horny."

Weston grinned.

"I want you to understand that it's just sex. You aren't my boyfriend and this isn't a relationship. We aren't going to hang out together. We'll be friendly, sure, but that's it. When we hookup it's just about getting off."

"Okay."

Weston sounded disappointed which confirmed my suspicions. He wanted more, but he wasn't getting it from me. If he wanted a boyfriend he would have to look elsewhere. He was cute and he was sexy, but he was no Caleb.

"Are you and Caleb..."

"It's none of your business, but right now we're close friends and very soon we'll probably be more. I'll be *very* angry if you try to hook up with him."

Weston didn't look happy at all.

"Be happy with what you've got," I said. "Do you know how many guys are dying to sleep with me? Do you have any idea? If you're willing to be here when I want to fuck, fine, but if you aren't happy with that..."

"No. No. It's great! Thank you! I... I didn't think I had a chance with you, but...well, this is a dream come true for me."

I grinned. He sounded like he was getting ready to fall to his knees and kiss my feet. I liked that.

"Okay. I think we understand each other. Now, I have some work to do before my first class so you need to leave."

Weston stood.

"Thanks for the coffee and even more for last night. I left my number by the bed. If you want me..."

"If I want you, I'll call you," I said.

Weston nodded, turned, and left. I poured myself some more coffee, sat at the table, and grinned.

Chapter Seven: A Date with Caleb

I stopped by Daulton's studio in the evening. I knew he would be quite hurt if I didn't spend some time with him and quite delighted if I showed up unannounced. Unknown to anyone but Daulton I had my own key, so I let myself in and surprised him in the garden where he was capturing wild daisies on canvas.

"Dorian!" he said, dropping his brush and hugging me hard. "I've missed you!"

"It hasn't been that long, Daulton. This is my first week of classes, I've been terribly busy, but I wanted to come and see your latest project."

"Projects you mean. You know I move from one to the next as my mood sways me. Today has been so gorgeous I just had to paint some flowers. Please, sit and talk to me while I work. You know you inspire me by your mere presence. Your influence will allow me to make what would have been a good painting into a great work."

I smiled. Same old Daulton. I did rather like him. He was easily excited, eccentric, and hopelessly enamored of me.

"You are looking especially well today, Dorian."

"I've met someone."

I knew Daulton would be terribly jealous when I told him about Caleb and I must admit I took a sadistic pleasure in tormenting him with my tale of the brilliant young actor who had captured my heart. The guilt I should have felt was neutralized by the knowledge that Daulton would have been more hurt had I not told him.

Daulton desired me, but he knew he could never have me, not so much because I would not yield to him, but because he himself prevented it. Daulton had so idealized me that he couldn't allow himself to taint that vision by actually sleeping with me. I found his logic quite bizarre and irrational, but I could see that it made perfect sense to Daulton, if to no one else.

I could not help but torment Daulton with the tale of the drunk wrestler I'd seduced or the story of popping Weston's cherry.

"This is all Seth's doing. I wish the two of you had never met. Seth has been a great friend to me and a patron of my art, but he is a terrible influence."

"Seth merely opened my eyes to the truth. He did tell me the truth, you know. The world does fall at my feet now, but before long it will cease to do so. I am doing no more than seizing the moment."

"Seizing the moment, yes, but look what you're doing, Dorian. You are in love with Caleb and yet you...sleep with other boys and with one that is a classmate of you both no less! How can you say you love him when you cheat on him so?"

"I'm not cheating on him. We aren't dating yet and so I cannot cheat on him. I'm moving slowly with him because I love and respect him. Weston and the others, they're nothing to me. They are pleasurable diversions. They are outlets for my sexual needs. Nothing more. Once Caleb and I become a couple there will be no other in my life. All those who desire me will look upon Caleb and me with despair because they will know that we belong to each other and to no one else."

"If you truly loved him you would save yourself for him, Dorian."

"You are far too old fashioned, Daulton. You are not yet thirty and yet you talk like an old man. No one saves themselves for marriage anymore, not even girls. Females were the ones who suffered the most under that old fashioned idea. While it was understood that men would get some on the sly, women were expected to wait for their wedding night. What a horrible injustice and here you are, wanting me to act like some Victorian bride. This is the twentieth century and there is no girl in our relationship. If there were it certainly wouldn't be me."

"What if Caleb thinks as you do? What if he's sleep around with other boys?"

"I sincerely doubt he does, but if he does that is his business. I must admit I don't like the idea of anyone else touching him. I consider him mine, but he is not yet truly mine and so he is free to do as he pleases."

"I don't think you mean that last part. I don't think you mean it at all. I think you would be terribly jealous if you found out Caleb slept with someone else and terribly angry too. You sleep with whomever you please, but you want him to wait for you."

"You are right about one thing," I said.

"What's that?"

"That I sleep with whoever I please."

"Dorian! I don't know why I put up with you. You're incorrigible and that too is Seth's fault."

"You would lay the troubles of the world at Seth's feet. No, as I've told you before Seth merely opened my eyes to the truth. When I am old and wrinkled and gray and the world no longer loves me at least I will know I lived life to the fullest. I fucked all the boys I wanted, I flirted all I wanted, and I broke all the heart's I wanted. I'll at least have the satisfaction of that and lots of good memories."

Daulton shook his head and painted in silence for a while. I grinned. I loved to irritate him, but I'd told him nothing but the truth.

We chatted about less explosive topics. I talked more than Daulton because he tended to become absorbed in his work. When he had painted my portrait he had barely spoken at all. He was freer with his words while painting in his garden. Perhaps daisies took less concentration.

I walked around so that I could see his progress after we'd been talking a good, long while.

"Daulton! It's absolutely beautiful. I must have it. I'll pay you a thousand dollars for it."

"This? I've painted this in an afternoon. It's a mere diversion."

"It's a wonderful work of art from a great artist."

"You flatter me. If you want it you may have it. I will give it to you."

"No. I will pay you. Art is your occupation as well as your passion and you can't pay the bills by giving away your creations. You would not let me pay for my portrait and Seth would have given you thousands for it. You must let me pay you for this. I have mountains of money and I consider a thousand dollars a great bargain for such a wonderful work of art."

"If you insist. I need more art lovers like you, those with deep pockets who don't mind overpaying."

"I have deep pockets, but you underestimate the value of your art. You are truly talented, Daulton. I greatly admire you. I'll tell you something now, but if you repeat it I'll deny it. I'm jealous of your talent."

"Dorian, it is completely absurd that you are jealous of me in any way. There are many who would sell their souls to look like you."

"Regardless, I am jealous. I will mail you a check and I shall not come to see you again until you cash it. I mean it, Daulton."

"Very well. I will submit to your blackmail, as you knew I would. There, it is finished."

"It's only finished after you sign it."

Daulton did so with a flourish. It was a great work of art. Looking at it made me feel like summer. I knew just what I was going to do with it. It would be a gift for Caleb. He would love it.

"Once it's dried, varnished, and framed I'll have it delivered to you," Daulton said.

"I'll be excited to receive it."

I lingered with Daulton, both because I knew it would please him and because I'd always enjoyed the company of talented people. Artists, writers, musicians, and particularly actors—I loved them all. I so wished I could be artist myself, but I realized I could not have it all.

When I left it was late and I walked leisurely through downtown and then across campus. The first thing I did when I returned to Read was to write Daulton a check and stick it in the mail. I couldn't wait to receive the painting so I could give it to Caleb.

***

I was prepared for my acting class audition, but I was sure I wasn't as well prepared as Caleb. I sat beside him as we were called up one by one just as we would have been for a Broadway audition, only here our only judge was our professor. I was called before Caleb. I was slightly nervous, not because I feared I'd mess up or not get the part, but because Caleb was watching. Once I started I could feel myself meld into the character. As I interacted with the student reading with me, I pretended that he was Caleb playing the part of J. Pierrepont Finch. When I finished, Caleb smiled at me proudly.

I had been so focused on Caleb and my audition since the beginning of class that I'd failed to notice Weston. It was the first time I'd seen him since I'd taken his virginity. He blushed slightly when he looked at me. I winked and he grinned.

I turned my attention back to Caleb. He was called to audition and I watched as he walked up onto the stage. He had the hottest ass.

I sat there mesmerized as Caleb performed what I thought of as the most difficult scene for his character. It was a scene from near the end of the play where everything falls apart and J. Pierrepont Finch uses desperate and elegant persuasion to save not only himself, but the President of the company and everyone else. Caleb pulled it off flawlessly He was so very talented he didn't need scenery or even other actors. When he finished I was disorientated for a moment. I was so pulled in I expected the play to continue. Caleb was *that* incredible.

After class, Weston eyed me, but he saw me with Caleb so he didn't approach. I was glad he knew where he stood with me. Caleb and I talked enthusiastically and I was surprised that he was so excited about my performance.

"You were wonderful, Dorian."

"I did well, but you, Caleb...when you finished I didn't even know where I was again. I actually expected the play to continue." I laughed. "You are truly, truly talented and I love you for it."

I leaned in and kissed him on the lips. We were in a fairly crowded hallway and I did not care. I wanted everyone to know that Caleb was mine.

"You haven't forgotten our date tonight, have you?" I asked.

"Of course not, but I can't spend the afternoon with you. I have work to finish and I have to get ready for this evening."

"I appreciate any time I have with you. I shall not be greedy," I said.

"You're so good to me, Dorian."

"Where would you like to go this evening?"

"Anywhere. Nowhere. It doesn't matter."

I grinned. I had the feeling Caleb cared for me as much as I did him.

"Then, I shall surprise you. When can you meet me?"

"I should say eight so I can get more done, but there is no way I can wait that long. I'll just have to spend more of my Saturday studying. Six?"

"I'll pick you up in front of Teter at six then."

"I can't wait!"

"I'll walk you to your dorm."

"I'm going to Wells Library, but you can walk me there."

We had a pleasant if short walk together. I said goodbye to him at the south entrance. We hugged, then kissed. I walked back the long way, through the Arboretum. My head was in the clouds and everything was so beautiful. I could feel other students gazing at me as I passed, but I was in my own little world. Nothing mattered but Caleb. As I walked toward Read I began to plan a wonderful evening for us.

I thought of just where to take Caleb. I detoured toward my new destination, quickly fulfilled my mission, and walked back toward Read secure in the knowledge that the main part of our evening was set. What's more, I knew Caleb would enjoy it.

Despite the level of excitement running through my body, I forced myself to do some of my own schoolwork. I intended to attend the game on Saturday so I wanted to get at least some of my work cleared away so it would not haunt my weekend. Besides, it was better than pacing the floor and watching the clock.

The time did pass quickly for me and that was my true goal. I simply could not wait until I could be with Caleb again. I put my books away at half past five, showered, and then dressed in khaki shorts and a deep purple polo. I thought of wearing long pants, but this was summer and there was no need to be formal, even though I'd planned for a very nice evening.

Just before six I walked outside and climbed into the Jag. I put the top down and drove up to Teter Quad. I pulled into the half-circle drive and waited only a minute before Caleb appeared looking so very handsome in khaki shorts similar to mine and an emerald green polo that matched his eyes. He slipped into the passenger side, leaned over, and kissed me on the lips.

"Where are you taking me?" he asked.

"First to Grazie. I know you love Italian."

"It sounds wonderful."

I drove us down to the square and found a parking spot right across from the Grazie Italian Eatery on Sixth Street. We walked across the street and were soon seated on the outdoor patio where we could talk, eat, and watch passersby.

I ordered a spinach and artichoke al forno appetizer when the waiter came for our drink orders. An artichoke dip might not sound tasty, but I knew from experience it was wonderful. Caleb and I browsed through our menus and were ready to order when our waiter brought our Cokes. Caleb ordered eggplant parmesan and I ordered lasagna al forno.

"I love eating at a table outside when it's beautiful like this," Caleb said. "I'm a people watcher."

"You're no doubt stealing mannerisms and accents from passersby for future characters."

Caleb stared at me for a moment.

"How did you know that?"

"Because you are a dedicated actor. You put everything you have into it. You don't think of it as an occupation. If you had more money than you could ever spend, you'd still be doing exactly what you're doing because you love to act."

"You're right."

"Take these auditions for example. I did the best I could, but what I put into preparing was nothing compared to what you put into it. You have a rare level of dedication, passion, and love for acting."

"You have no idea how much it means to have someone who understands, Dorian. My family has never understood. They are putting me through college and for that I'm grateful, but I know they're hoping I'm discover some other passion. I even overheard my dad tell my mom that even if I was wasting my time acting I'd still come out with a good education that I could put to use in finding a *real* job."

"He'll change his mind when he sees your name in foot-high letters on a marquee on Broadway or when he walks into a movie theater and reads your name on the screen."

"Do you really think that will happen, Dorian?"

"I know it will."

We sat and watched people walking by; college students, middle-age couples, high school kids, and senior citizens. I loved the square in downtown Bloomington in the summer. Unlike most downtowns this one was alive and bustling. There were several restaurants on the square, two bookstores, and numerous little shops, including an art gallery and gourmet cooking store. Bike traffic was considerable. There were more bicycles in Bloomington than I'd seen in any other town. Part of that was no doubt due to IU. The campus was large and a bike made for quick transportation. It was also much easier to find parking for a bike.

Flowers grew in boxes along the street and trees beautified the square. Bloomington was a lovely town. I knew I'd made the right choice when I'd chosen IU.

I looked across the table at Caleb and grasped his hand. The best part about coming to Bloomington was finding Caleb. I had no doubt it was destiny. I knew this boy would change my life forever.

We sat and talked, mostly about theater of course, until our food arrived and then we talked more. We took our time. There was no hurry. My lasagna was delicious. I suggested dessert, but Caleb said he was far too full. I was as well.

We lingered over coffee while I kept an eye on the time. After a few minutes more I paid the check and led Caleb not toward the car, but across and down the street to Kirkwood. Caleb didn't ask where we were going, but just let me lead him. As we neared the Buskirk Chumley Theater I pulled a pair of tickets out of my pocket.

"Oh! I've been wanting to see this, Dorian!"

I grinned to see Caleb so excited. I'd purchased tickets earlier to the evening performance of Sweeney Todd.

We entered and took our seats. I'd timed our arrival so we wouldn't have a long wait before the performance began. We browsed through our programs and looked around at the old theater. Maybe I'd buy my own theater someday and stage productions with Caleb as the star.

The play began. Caleb sat mesmerized. I enjoyed the play immensely, but I watched Caleb almost as much as the action on the stage. I thoroughly enjoyed watching his reactions and unbounded enthusiasm for the performance.

Other patrons gazed at us from time to time. I was accustomed to drawing attention, but now that I was with Caleb I enjoyed the attention more. I didn't hesitate to sit close, wrap my arm around him, or take his hand.

I had always enjoyed theater, but with Caleb sitting beside me I loved it even more. To share such an experience was to increase the enjoyment of it exponentially. Caleb improved my life merely by being a part of it.

The production was wonderful. I was quite sure Caleb could have performed any of the parts better than those on stage, but I was a little biased. The actors did a superb job, the sets made me feel like I was in London, and the lighting made me forget I was sitting inside a darkened theatre. A good play like this one was a magical experience.

Caleb hugged me under the marquee after the show was over. He was absolutely delighted and I was just as delighted that I could make him so very happy. We walked back to the Jag and I drove him to Read.

"Come inside with me. I have a surprise for you," I said. "It won't take long, I promise."

I let Caleb into my suite. He looked around with wide eyes.

"*This* is your dorm room?"

"It's meant to be shared, but I managed to get it all to myself and I made a few...improvements."

"It's more like a luxury hotel suite than a college dorm. How...I don't think I'll ask. This is quite a surprise."

"It's not the one I mentioned. This is your surprise," I said, handing Caleb a large, flat, rectangular package wrapped in plain brown paper.

Caleb opened the package to reveal the painting of daisies I had so recently purchased from Daulton.

"Dorian. I don't know what to say. It's incredible!"

"It was just delivered late this afternoon. I know the artist. He was working on it when I visited his studio and I just had to have it for you."

"I love it, but this is too..."

"Don't say it. It makes me happy to give it to you. It's as much a gift for me as it is for you."

Caleb put the painting down for a moment, hugged me and kissed me. I hesitated to let him go, but if I knew if I didn't things would go too far. I intended to make love with Caleb, but at the right time. It was too soon in our romance to fall into bed together.

I gave Caleb another peck and then walked him outside. I took his hand and we walked together toward Teter Quad. It was a beautiful night and I couldn't recall being quite so happy before. I kissed Caleb again in front of Teter.

"Thank you for tonight, it was wonderful," Caleb said.

"Thank you."

"I love this painting. I don't know what to say."

I leaned in and kissed him one more time.

"See you soon?" I asked.

"Definitely."

I walked home alone in the darkness, or what darkness there was with all the street lights. Campus was will-lit. I felt safe and secure here.

When I returned to Read, I undressed and climbed into bed. I lay with my arms behind my back and ran through the events of the evening in my mind. I smiled. It had been one incredible night.

Chapter Eight:
Playing with the Quarterback

I slept in Saturday morning, skipped breakfast, and hit the books. I steadily worked away until the phone rang a little before noon. I was surprised and delighted to hear Caleb's voice. My smile faded slightly as I spoke to him, but soon reappeared. After I said "goodbye" I picked my keys off the counter, walked out to my Jag, and drove to Teter Quad.

I could see Caleb standing with an older, more muscular version of himself. I would have known he was Caleb's brother even had I not been expecting him. He wasn't quite as good-looking as Caleb, but he had a hot body. I pulled up beside them.

"Dorian, this is my brother, James"

"It's very nice to meet you," I said.

James climbed into the back of the convertible and Caleb jumped in the front.

"Where to?" I asked.

"I think James would like Opie Taylors," Caleb said.

"Then Opie Taylors it is."

I drove downtown, which was not far distant. It was a beautiful day. The sun was shining brightly and the whole world was filled with life. I looked over at Caleb and we grinned at each other.

When we arrived at Opie Taylors, Caleb slid into one side of a booth with me and James took the other. Caleb sat close and even put his arm around my shoulder. James eyed me suspiciously, but he was friendly enough. Our waitress came and we placed our drink orders.

"I didn't know James was coming," Caleb said. "He surprised me. He also surprised me with his news." Caleb frowned.

"I'm going into the Navy soon and Caleb doesn't approve," James said.

"It's not that I don't approve. It's just that I don't like the idea of not seeing you for years at a time."

"There is such a thing as leave, little brother. We don't see each other for months at a time now. I'll still be able to call. It will be very little different from the way it is now. You're a big boy now. I think you can handle it."

Caleb stuck out his tongue. Suddenly, he was the mischievous little brother.

"You guys seem very close," I said.

"We are," Caleb said. "We shared the same room for years. I told James I was gay before I told anyone else."

"Like I didn't already know. When he was eleven he'd stare at underwear ads in catalogs and when he was thirteen he began collecting Undergear catalogs. Then, there were the show tunes and...well, it was just obvious."

"He was totally cool about it," Caleb said. "Things would have been a lot rougher for me if James hadn't been around. Having a big, tough, older brother helps keep the bullies away."

I smiled at James. I was beginning to like him.

"He even came to see all my plays."

"Stop," James said, but I could tell he was pleased.

"I never had a brother. I used to wish for one. Now, it's too late. You two are very lucky," I said.

"Caleb told me about your parents," James said. "He's told me a lot about you. In fact, when he calls, he won't shut up about you."

I could almost detect an unsaid, 'So I came to check you out.'

Our waitress returned with our drinks. I ordered a basil burger and fries. James ordered a Swiss and Jalapeno burger and fries. Caleb ordered a three-cheese cheeseburger and fries.

"When do you go into the Navy?" I asked.

"I leave for basic training in a week."

"Not long then."

"No. I'm looking forward to it. I almost went into the Navy when I was your age. I'm twenty-three now and time is slipping by. It's something I really want to pursue."

"Then you should. I'm a firm believer in doing what one wants. Sorry, Caleb."

"Don't worry about it. There's no changing his mind once he decides to do something."

We talked until our lunch arrived and then kept talking, only with frequent pauses for eating. A picture formed in my mind of an older jock looking out for his gay little brother and his little brother idolizing him in return. I could see why Caleb didn't want him to go into the Navy. Caleb wasn't a little boy anymore, but knowing his big brother wasn't and couldn't be there for him probably made him feel insecure. He'd be okay. He had me now. I didn't have James's muscles, but I was powerful in my own way. I would protect Caleb.

I dropped Caleb and James off at Teter after lunch. Caleb hugged and kissed me. His brother shook my hand, but I could feel he didn't quite trust me

I drove back to Read and studied some more. My goal had been to get all my work out of the way before the game, but my unplanned lunch-date had made that unlikely. Regardless, I was quite pleased with myself for having the discipline to focus on schoolwork when scantily-clad young men were wandering about outside. If all went well this afternoon, I'd reward myself by bringing home a football player, ideally Brendan.

At about 2:30, I walked to the nearest bus stop and caught a campus bus to the stadium. I could have driven, but I knew traffic and parking would be a nightmare. Taking the bus was much easier and besides, it was packed with sexy college boys on their way to the game.

A pair of guys about my age were eyeing me and whispering to each other. They were definitely homos. I flirted with them just for fun and even winked as I got off the bus.

There was an enormous crowd all around the stadium. Tailgating was a big tradition. There were tents and folding tables set up all over near the parked cars. There were even food stands offering all kinds of things. I wandered around, bought myself a Coke, and enjoyed the pre-game atmosphere. I didn't even bother to look for Brendan. I was sure he was already in the locker room. Even if he was walking around outside there is no way I could have spotted him among the hundreds and hundreds of fans.

Across 17th Street was an even bigger tailgate party. There must have been at least five hundred students milling around, drinking, talking, dancing, and laughing. The street was jam packed with cars entering the parking lots. It would have been impossible to get across, but the traffic often slowed to a complete stop and the campus police sometimes stopped traffic to let pedestrians cross. There were throngs of students walking along both sides of the street. There were people everywhere!

I crossed the street to check out the party. Most everyone was wearing a crimson IU shirt of one design or another. I wore one myself and was soon lost in a crimson sea. Girls and guys checked me out. I smiled and flirted and enjoyed being looked at. Wherever I walked I drew attention and I ate it up. I spotted several boys I wanted to do, but I had no time for seduction now. Besides, I had a special conquest in mind. I wanted Brendan Brewer.

As game-time neared I followed the masses back across the street and into the stadium parking lots. I found my gate and walked down to my seat. I had scored a great vantage point to watch the game.

I wasn't a sports fan, but I was a fan of athletic young men. When the IU team took the field they looked hunky and delicious in their red and white uniforms. I loved the pants they wore; they were so tight and revealing. The shoulder pads and jerseys left everything to the imagination, but I knew most of the players had to be buff.

The players looked a lot alike from the stadium seats. I had no idea which one of them was Brendan. For all I knew he wasn't even on the field. I still enjoyed the game. Football is very homoerotic and voyeuristic. Think about it. Thousands of people, mostly guys, watching as young jocks show off their athletic prowess and jump on each other. It was just this side of porn. I wondered what all the "straight" football fans would think about that. Personally, I thought every male football fan displayed latent homosexuality at the very least.

I realized something as I sat there with thousands of others watching the game. My chances of crossing Brendan's path were slim. I would have had a much better chance staking out his dorm. When the crowd headed out of the stadium there would be a flood of people everywhere and the players likely made themselves scarce.

Some of the college boys near me pulled off their shirts and I was distracted. Guys with muscles really turned me on. Hunks weren't usually all that bright, but I wasn't interested in their minds. I could never date a jock, but I could sure take one back to my suite and make use of his hot body.

I didn't get wrapped up in the game like everyone else, but I enjoyed it. I probably wouldn't bother to come to another, but I wanted to watch at least one. I was carried along by the excitement of the crowd and there was plenty of eye candy both in the stands and on the field to make the game worthwhile.

It was probably futile, but I lingered after the game to try to spot Brendan. At first, there were such an enormous crowd I probably wouldn't have noticed him if he passed within ten feet of me. As the crowd thinned, I had a chance of picking him out, but the Memorial Stadium was huge and had several exits. He could leave by any of them. For all I knew, he already had.

I didn't find Brendan. I wandered around the stadium until almost everyone had left and there was no sign of him. Most likely he'd headed out already. I sighed. I hated disappointment and I'd been fantasizing about taking him back to my suite and getting it on.

I was just turning to leave when I caught sight not of Brendan, but of an extremely handsome and well-built young stud. He was about 6'3" and all muscle with curly black hair and piercing blue eyes. He noticed me at almost the same time I did him. His expression was appraising and hungry. I smiled seductively.

The young god walked toward me.

"If you came for the game, you're a little late," he said.

"I saw it."

"Football fan?"

"I'm not a fan of football, just the players."

"Oh really?"

"Yes. You look like you could play football."

"I do."

"Yeah? So I probably just watched you running around on the field."

"I'm sure you did. I'm Gabrial. I'm the quarterback."

Any sports fan would have recognized the quarterback of the IU football team, but not me. I didn't follow football and, like I said, all the players looked alike down on the field.

I hadn't found Brendan, but I had found a football player, and the quarterback no less. There was still time to salvage my plans for the night.

"I'm Dorian. You're very...athletic, Gabrial."

"And not just on the field. So...what are you doing this evening?"

"I'm taking the quarterback to my place."

Gabrial smiled and closed in until he was almost on top of me.

"You seem very sure of yourself."

"I am."

"I like that, but let's alter the plan slightly. My car is parked just outside. Why don't I drive us to your place?"

"I like that change."

Gabrial led me to his car, a cherry red Trans Am. It suited his personality and fit with his look, just as my Jag did mine. I directed him to drive to Read and soon we had parked and entered the dorm.

I was accustomed to people gazing at me, but they looked at Gabrial and me together even more. They were no doubt wondering what we were doing together. If they only knew...

"This is it," I said, stepping inside and locking the door behind us.

"Holy shit this is nice! I hope your roommates are out."

"I don't have roommates."

"All this is yours? Damn!

"I'm glad you like my place, but did you really come here to admire the furniture?" I grinned.

Gabrial turned to me, grabbed me and kissed me deeply.

I liked to seduce and control, but I was aroused this football hunk taking the lead. I admired strength, power, and aggression and Gabrial had all three. He kissed me roughly, probing deeply with his tongue. My body immediately responded and I was consumed by lust.

We slipped off our shoes and socks, then pulled off each other's shirts. Gabrial had the most fantastic body I'd ever seen in real life. Usually, bodies like his were seen only on the covers of magazines. He had a beautifully sculpted torso with powerful pecs, defined abs, and not an ounce of fat anywhere.

"You are fucking beautiful," Gabrial said as he ran his hands over my smooth, firm chest.

Gabrial leaned down and licked my nipples, sending a shiver through my body. I knew already that he would be as talented in bed as he was on the football field.

We moved toward my bedroom, leaving a trail of clothing behind. By the time we fell onto my bed we were both completely naked. Gabrial was all over me, licking and kissing and sucking. He pulled me into his mouth and I moaned. He worked me into a writhing mass of ecstasy.

When Gabrial rolled onto his side I pounced on him and explored his body from head to foot. I went down on him and outdid myself in giving him pleasure. He moaned and groaned and grasped the sheets in his hands.

We made out and rolled over each other, feeling and fondling. Gabrial slipped off the bed for a moment and when he turned back he was holding a condom and looking at me like he was a tiger and I was a gazelle. He slipped on the condom, pulled my legs up over his shoulders and entered me.

I expected pain, but there wasn't any. I don't know how he did it but from that first moment there was only pleasure.

"Oh—fuck—yes!" I moaned loudly.

Gabrial pounded me. It should have hurt. I should have been begging him to stop or fighting him off, but the experience was pure pleasure. I urged him on and he went at it harder and harder until he was panting and sweating, athlete though he was. After I few minutes my body convulsed, I cried out in ecstasy, and exploded in sticky pleasure even though neither of us had touched me. Gabrial went deep and hard, then moaned loudly.

He pulled out and then lay by me on his back, gasping for breath.

"That was the most awesome sex I've ever had in my life," Gabrial said. "You are so fucking beautiful and sexy, damn!"

"I was going to say the same to you," I said with a grin. "I almost never bottom and that didn't hurt at all. It was pure pleasure."

"I guess that means you'll want me to come back."

"I've never said this to a guy before, but you can come back anytime you want."

"You're a 'love them and leave them' type, huh?" Gabrial said.

"I'm a fuck them and leave them type, but you... just *damn!*"

"I think we're a lot alike, Dorian. I think we're going to get along just fine."

***

My night with Gabrial was only the first of many. We created a stir on campus when we walked together. I would have thought Gabrial would want to keep things on the down-low, but he was obviously an attention-whore also. We didn't hold hands or kiss in public as I did with Caleb. Gabrial and I didn't have that kind of relationship. Ours was based purely on mutual attraction and sex. There was no emotional bond. We were both hedonist and we respected each other for our self-confidence and for our powers of seduction.

I discovered from Gabrial that his teammate, Brendan, was gay, but that he was devoted to a boyfriend back home. Gabrial told me of his long range plan to seduce Brendan. I was impressed and I agreed with him than Brendan's long-distance relationship wouldn't last. I decided to back off for the moment and not actively pursue Brendan. If our paths crossed, fine, but if not I'd wait. Time would only make seducing him easier. The poor boy didn't stand a chance. Two of the hottest guys on campus were determined to have him. It was only a matter of who got into his pants first. Gabrial had a clear advantage. Brendan was his teammate and saw him often. I almost never saw him at all. I was still confident. Sooner or later I'd have him even if Gabrial got to him first. Perhaps, we'd have him together.

I didn't mind not having Brendan. I had Gabrial and there were others as well. Weston gazed at me longingly during classes. I had him several times during the following weeks. He knew he was nothing but a toy to me, something to use and discard, but he never once denied me when I wanted him. He served me whenever I needed him and thanked me for the opportunity. I must admit I was a bit cruel to him, but then that's exactly what he wanted and needed. He craved it and I satisfied his need even as I sated my own lust. From the outside ours would have appeared an abusive relationship, but it was symbiotic. I really didn't care. As long as I got what I wanted I was content.

I didn't have much time for seducing other boys and that was fine by me because I was spending a great deal of time with Caleb. In fact, neither of us did much beyond attending classes, studying, and spending time together. I took him out to one restaurant after another until Caleb asked if I intended to take him to them all. I bought him flowers, a gold chain and matching bracelet, books and music. He protested until he learned that I was going to buy him things whether he liked it or not. He surrendered, ceased protesting, and thanked me with a hug and a kiss. I think he finally understood that I loved to spoil him. What was money worth if I couldn't spend it on someone I adored?

Chapter Nine: The Proposal

We were several weeks into our relationship and the fall semester was speeding by. The furthest we had gone was some very heavy making out and groping. I could not have denied myself sex with Caleb for so very long if I hadn't been getting it on regularly with Gabrial, Weston, and occasionally another random boy. Even with the release I found with others I longed for Caleb. I knew he wanted me. I could read it in his eyes and his body gave away the secrets of his lust. The time was at hand for us to finally take off our clothes and make love, but our first time had to be special.

I had been bouncing around ideas for weeks. A spectacular evening would not be long enough, so I planned a spectacular Saturday instead. The waiting was agonizing, but finally the long-awaited day arrived. I told Caleb to clear his schedule for Saturday. Nothing could be allowed to interrupt us.

We started our day with a visit to the IU art museum and gazed at the paintings and Greek, Roman, and Egyptian artifacts. We strolled around campus, stopping often to make out. I had a difficult time calming myself because I was bursting to give Caleb his biggest gift yet. I had to force myself to wait.

We had lunch at an outdoor table at the Runcible Spoon near campus and just down the street from the Monroe County library. We sat at a table with an umbrellas overhead. There were flowers growing all around. Small birds pecked at scraps fallen from tables. It was almost as if we were dining in a forest and yet we were only feet from Sixth Street. I ordered the Tex/Mex omelet which was made with avocado, sour cream, Colby cheese, tomatoes, and ranchero salsa. Caleb ordered gypsy chicken with rosemary potatoes.

"My brother asked about you," Caleb said as we sipped our Cokes and waited on our orders.

"Still suspicious after all this time?"

"He thinks you're too good to be true. You are, of course, but I know you are true. He's just waiting for something to happen. I only tell him about a few of the things you buy me. I don't dare tell him about them all or he'd be sure you were up to something."

"Oh, I am up to something. I intend to seduce you."

"You already have. You have charmed me at any rate. If you mean seduce as in making-love, then I'd say it's about time."

I grinned.

"It is definitely time," I said.

Caleb looked as if he wanted to leap across the table and pounce on me. I had to readjust myself because my shorts were suddenly much too tight.

Our food arrived. I nearly moaned when I tasted mine and not because I was all worked up thinking about making love with Caleb. It was the best omelet I had ever tasted. It was also the most beautiful. The outside was mostly covered with dark, green leaves of some herb or salad green I could not identify.

"This is incredible," Caleb said. "I think we should have tried this place sooner."

"No wonder it's so crowded when I walk by," I said. "I've never had an omelet this delicious before."

We paid more attention to eating than talking for a while and that was fine with both of us. Just being together was enough and I had much on my mind. I had trouble just sitting still. My ability to contain myself was slipping.

"What are you so excited about?" Caleb asked me as we ate.

"I have a surprise for you, but...I can't tell you about it yet."

"Oh, Dorian. You've done so much for me already."

I just smiled.

"Tell me more about play practice," I said, trying to distract us both.

Our practice auditions in class had moved onto the real thing. I was beaten out for my part by another more talented actor. I wasn't surprised or particularly disappointed. Caleb had won the lead role for the fall production of *How To Succeed In Business Without Really Trying* with his superior acting abilities. That was no surprise either. I knew he'd do it. Since he was in the cast and I was not I'd mostly lost touch with the production. I was currently giving a hand with costume design (and being much assisted in that by Daulton) and had no interaction with the actors outside of class.

"It's going fairly well, it's just..."

"What?"

"Sometimes I just don't feel the role. I feel like I'm...acting."

"Well, you are acting, Caleb."

"Yes, but I never feel like I'm acting. I feel as if I am the character I'm playing."

"You know you'll do an excellent job. You always have in the past, right?"

Caleb nodded.

"So stop worrying. You are the most talented actor I have ever had the privilege to watch, let alone know, and I adore you for it. After this fall's performance, all of Bloomington will know of your talent and soon the whole world will fall at your feet."

"I don't know about that last bit, but you're right. I'll do fine. I always get the jitters when we're closing in on the actual performance and I always worry about nothing."

"Exactly, so knock it off," I said with a grin. "As for the rest, perhaps you can't see it, but you are truly a great actor, Caleb. Someday, those who know you now will brag to their friends that they went to school with Caleb Black."

Caleb smiled and shook his head.

"You're incorrigible."

"What I am is absolutely right."

We finished our lunch and then I drove Caleb over to College Avenue and turned south.

"Where are you we going?"

"To pick up your surprise. I simply cannot wait a moment longer."

I could tell Caleb didn't have a clue, but then I'd expected that.

"Isn't the Humane Shelter down this way? You didn't get me a puppy did you? I can't have one in my dorm."

"I didn't get you a puppy."

"What did you get me?"

Caleb's curiosity was making him increasingly excited.

"You'll find out very soon."

I kept driving until we came to the GM Dealership. I pulled in.

"No way! Dorian, you didn't!"

"I did," I said and grinned.

"Dorian!"

"Don't start protesting. I've already bought it and you're accepting it. I shall be very hurt if you don't and I'll never forgive you."

"Please tell me it's used at least...and old."

I shook my head.

"Dorian!"

I laughed.

"I knew this would be fun," I said.

I pulled around to the side and parked.

"Wait here," I said.

I went in and got the keys from the dealer. He shook my hand. Soon, I was back in the Jag with Caleb.

"It's in the back," I said.

We drove around the back and there it was, sitting all alone with a big red ribbon and bow over the hood—a new 1983 Trans Am convertible in bright, metallic blue.

"Oh. My. God," Caleb said, staring at it. His mouth dropped open and he went speechless.

I got out of the car. Caleb just sat in the passenger side, gaping. I had to go around, open the door, and pull him out. I led him forward. He just stared.

"Dorian," he said. Tears ran down his cheeks.

He turned to me and hugged me tightly.

"I can't believe you bought me a car!" he said when he released me. "Dorian! You really should not have..."

"Shh," I said, placing my finger over his lips. "No arguments or objections are allowed."

I took my finger away and kissed him. I handed Caleb the keys.

"Meet me back at Read. I'll leave the Jag there and you can drive me around in your new car."

Caleb wiped tears away. He was actually crying and smiling at the same time. I climbed back into the Jag and drove off so he wouldn't have a chance to argue.

I had to wait by my Jag for a few minutes after I got back to Read. No doubt Caleb was driving slowly in his new car. I grinned. Giving the car to him had given me an enormous amount of pleasure. I loved what money could buy.

Caleb pulled up and I climbed into the passenger side. It's about time you started chauffeuring *me* around for a change," I said. "Drive me somewhere."

Caleb pulled out and did just that.

"I can't believe you bought me a car. I never expected this."

Caleb repeated the first sentence several times in the next few days and I grinned every time he said it.

We drove slowly around the streets of Bloomington, past businesses and through residential areas. Both of us saw parts of Bloomington we'd never seen before. Caleb drove us around for a hour, then I asked him to pull into the parking lot of the Chocolate Moose. I ordered a hot caramel sundae and Caleb ordered a marshmallow shake. We leaned against the Trans Am and ate.

The Chocolate Moose had some of the best ice cream in Bloomington. Whenever I was in the mood for ice cream, I headed there.

Two college boys came over and admired Caleb's car. He was delighted to tell them it was his. He was extremely proud of it and that made me smile. My boyfriend, and I was beginning to think of Caleb as exactly that, deserved to drive around in a sharp car.

I was ready to get serious with Caleb. I intended to propose to him shortly, not marriage of course, but a serious, committed relationship. I'd have to give up Gabrial and Weston, give up the idea of seducing Brendan, and give up all the random sexual encounters that satisfied my lust, but I was ready. I'd thought about it and Caleb was worth it. He was theater personified. I was completely in awe of his talent and I wanted to be there to watch his star rise.

We finished our ice cream and headed back to Read. I led Caleb inside and into my suite. He had been there before, but we'd never spent a lot of time there. I was always afraid that I'd lose control if I was with him alone for too long a period of time. I wanted to wait until the time was right and now the moment had come.

I poured Caleb a glass of wine and we drank as we stood at the window and admired the view.

"I have one thing more for you today," I said.

"Oh, Dorian."

"It's for us really."

I took his wine and placed both glasses on a table. I kneeled down in front of him and pulled out a small black box covered with velvet. Caleb put his hand over his mouth and looked as if he might cry. I pulled out a pair of simple gold rings.

"Caleb Black, will you be my boyfriend?"

"Yes!" he said and began to softly cry.

Caleb pulled me to my feet and kissed me. I slipped the ring on his finger. He took the other ring from the box and slipped it on mine. We kissed again and held each other tight.

"You've made me so happy, Dorian."

"As you have me by saying 'yes'."

We hugged and kissed and I gently led Caleb to my bedroom. I moved slowly, giving him time to object, but he didn't resist. I kissed him again and slowly pulled his shirt over his head. Caleb was beautiful. He was slim and defined and firm. Caleb pulled my own shirt away and we kissed as we pressed our bare chests together.

We pulled off our shoes and socks, then kissed again, rubbing our crotches together. Caleb was clearly aroused. I unfastened his belt and unbuttoned his jeans. Caleb grasped my wrists and stopped me.

"I'm uh...I'm not big...down there," he said and turned crimson.

"I don't care," I said slowly and softly. "I don't care."

I nuzzled his neck and kissed him again. I unzipped his jeans and he didn't try to stop me. I pushed his jeans down and let them fall to the floor. Our movements became more urgent even as our breath quickened. Caleb tore through my own belt and buttons and shoved my jeans to the floor. We kicked our pants away and pressed hard into each other as we made out.

Caleb surprised me by jerking down my boxer-briefs. I stripped his away and we made out naked, rubbing against each other.

Caleb surprised me again by pushing me onto my back on the bed. He lowered his lips to my chest and kissed and licked me all over. He sucked on my nipples and I gasped. He was all over my entire torso, but didn't go down any further. When his lips met mine Caleb had worked me up so much that I grabbed his head and shoved my tongue into his mouth. We made out with fierce intensity, rolling around on my bed.

I pushed Caleb onto his back and mimicked his moves, driving him crazy by sucking on his small nipples. I kissed and licked all the way to his navel, but I didn't stop there. I leaned in and engulfed him.

Caleb wasn't big and I slid my lips all the way down to the base, making him moan loudly. I did my best to keep him moaning, using everything I'd learned from guys who'd gone down on me and putting all my practice at giving head to use. Caleb mattered more than all the others because he possessed a talent none of the others could touch.

One thing I'd learned was how to keep another guy from going over the edge. There were signs when a guy was getting close to orgasm. Some guys were moaners, others weren't. When a moaner began to get louder, he was getting close. When a non-moaner began to moan, he was about to shoot. Some guys never moaned at all, but their bodies still gave warning, as did the rate of their breathing. The faster the breath, the closer a guy was to exploding. Certain muscles in the groin tensed before an impending orgasm and if a guy's scrotum pulled up, he was about to lose control. I read Caleb's body as I worked to give him the most pleasure he'd ever experienced and when I sensed him getting close I pulled away, lay on top of him, and began to make out with him once more.

Caleb was more aggressive in bed than I'd anticipated, but I had no problem with that. I was aggressive and I loved being with other aggressive guys. What I didn't like were guys who were too passive and quiet, like the one I'd fucked a couple of weeks before. He didn't move or utter a sound. I couldn't tell if he liked it or not. After a couple of minutes of no reaction from him, I forgot all about him and focused on myself. I never bothered to return his calls.

I didn't have to think about other guys anymore. I had Caleb and I would be faithful to him. I'd fucked around until this day, but we'd made a commitment to each other and I would stand by it.

Caleb went down on me. He was good. He was *real* good. He couldn't take me all in. Unlike Caleb, I wasn't small. I wasn't what I'd call hung, but I was as big as most of the guys I'd hooked up with and bigger than some. It didn't matter. What mattered was the way Caleb went after it.

I just lay back and enjoyed myself. There was nothing quite so pleasurable as sex. After a few minutes, I had to pull Caleb's mouth up to mine or I would have totally lost control.

We made out and let our hands wander. I slowly pulled back from the brink. Caleb grinned at me and we kept kissing. Part of me wanted to go at it and finish, but most of me wanted to just keep going as we were. We took our time and thoroughly enjoyed ourselves. I thought about going all the way with Caleb, but I was so worked up that if I penetrated him I'd last all of ten seconds. Instead, I moved around until we were in a sixty-nine position.

I pulled Caleb into my mouth even as I felt him engulf me. We took it slowly, but our moans soon filled the room. Caleb began to thrust into me and I went at him harder. In moments, I felt his body convulse and he exploded in my mouth. That triggered my own orgasm and we lay there together moaning with our mouths full for what seemed like forever.

I pulled away and then lay beside Caleb. He scooted down and rested his head on my chest. I wrapped my arms around him and we lay there like that until we fell asleep.

I awakened later with my arms still around Caleb and with Caleb's head still on my chest. I sighed with contentment and then fell back asleep. I didn't awaken again until I felt Caleb stir the next morning.

I sat up on my elbows as Caleb scooted to the end of the bed. He stood, turned, then saw that I was awake.

"I thought I had a dream last night that you gave me a car, proposed to me, then we made love. Since we're both naked and I feel better than I have in ages, I guess it wasn't a dream."

I grinned. Caleb leaned over and kissed me on the lips.

"Mind if I take a shower?"

"Of course not. Everything you'll need is in the bathroom. I'll take one after you, then I'll take you out to breakfast."

"Can we go back to the Runcible Spoon? I want to celebrate our one day anniversary."

"We can do anything you want."

I lay there while Caleb showered, thinking about how my life had changed. I wondered what Seth would say when I told him I had committed to Caleb. Likely he say something about foolishly tying myself down when there were so many other guys out there, but it was Seth who encouraged me to live life to the fullest and go after what I wanted. What I wanted was Caleb.

I took my turn in the shower next. As I was drying off I realized Caleb didn't have any clean clothes. While most of yesterday had been planned and I'd hoped we would make love, I hadn't thought far enough ahead to consider Caleb spending the night. No matter. I'd run him by Teter and he could change. I wondered what his roommate would think about him staying out all night. I grinned.

I walked into the bedroom naked and dressed. Then, Caleb and I walked outside together. I'd momentarily forgotten he had a car. I climbed into the passenger side and Caleb drove us to his dorm. After a short wait, we were on our way again and were soon once more seated at a table under an umbrella at the Runcible Spoon.

"I feel like this is where it all started yesterday," Caleb said.

"At least it was the beginning of our main adventure. It was from here we departed to pick up your car."

"When you say you have a surprise, you aren't kidding," Caleb said.

I laughed.

We both ordered French toast, bacon, and coffee. We sat among the flowers and watched the birds foraging while we waited. When our French toast arrived it was heavenly.

"My brother was *so* wrong about you, but then I knew that all along," Caleb said.

"I'm glad you had no doubts."

"Never. No one has ever cared as much about me as you do."

I smiled.

"We're going to have a brilliant future together, Caleb. Soon, you'll be up on the stage showing everyone your talent. After college, you won't have to work at crummy jobs like most actors do while they're waiting for their big break. I'll support us. Then, after your first audition which will lead to a huge part you'll be a star and we'll live happily ever after."

"No one really lives happily ever after, though, do they?" Caleb said.

"No, but we're going to come closer than anyone ever has before."

Chapter Ten: Opening Night

November 1982

"Don't look at me like that, Daulton," Seth said. "All I said is that great romance leads to great tragedy. Look at Romeo & Juliet."

"Dorian and Caleb are entirely different. Isn't that right, Dorian?"

"That's exactly right," I said.

"Of course they are different! I'm talking about the basic concept of romance and the deep emotions involved. When deep emotions are in play they always lead tragedy."

"Don't say that," I begged.

"I'm sorry. I don't make up the rules. I'm just telling you both how it is."

"You're far too depressing, Seth," I said.

"I agree," Daulton said.

"Your agreement gives no weight to the argument," Seth said. "You are my friend, but you are often wrong, Daulton."

"When have I been wrong?"

"You said I'm a bad influence on Dorian. Just look at him. He's all dressed up to take us to his beloved's opening night. He has found his soul mate. Bad influence indeed!"

"I have to agree with Seth on that one," I said. "He has fired my passion for life. I don't think I would have pursued Caleb with such vigor if it had not been for Seth."

Seth took a bow.

"Yet he stands there and predicts doom."

"What of it, Daulton? You speak as if none of us should enjoy the journey when the destination is likely to be tragedy. It is the journey that is important! All life ends in tragedy. That tragedy is called death. If we were to follow your philosophy we'd all have to just lay down and die right now. I don't see how such a talented artist who creates such beautiful things can have such a gloomy view of life," I said.

"I don't have a gloomy view and you know it," Daulton said with a slight smile. "I just worry about you, Dorian."

"You worry too much," Seth said.

"Don't worry about me. I've never been happier. I am in love. Just wait until you see him perform! I tell you, Caleb is the greatest actor you will ever have the pleasure to watch and you'll be there at the very beginning. It is his talent that drew me to him and made me fall in love with him."

"We're expecting great things," Seth said. "I hope we aren't disappointed."

"You won't be."

Seth hired a car for the evening, so we were deposited right in front of the IU Auditorium. We were shown down front by a very handsome usher.

"These are excellent seats," Seth commented.

"Dating the star has its advantages," I said.

I was so excited I could barely sit still. I had waited so long for this night. It had been a tremendous temptation to slip in and watch a practice, but I had forced myself to stay away. My classes, schoolwork, and behind-the-scenes work with the wardrobe for the play had helped me avoid temptation by keeping me busy, but I still had idle hours. I had gone so far as to walk to the auditorium during play practice one evening, but had forced myself to turn around and go back to my dorm. I was so glad I possessed the self-disciple to wait.

Caleb was going to be brilliant. Everyone was going to love him. Seth and Daulton were going to adore him. I was taking everyone out after the performance. This was going to be the perfect theatrical night.

My heart beat faster as the performance began. It was beautifully staged and the actors, some of whom I recognized from class, impressed me. I took special note of the costumes. My part in their design and production was minor, but still I noticed a bit of my work here and there. I glanced at Daulton. I could see that he noticed that some of his suggestions had been utilized. I knew he was pleased.

When Caleb stepped onto the stage I forgot about everything else. He was so handsome all attention was immediately and naturally focused on him. He spoke his first line...

I frowned slightly. Something was off. I couldn't understand, but something was not right. I was thrown and my attention diverted to my own thoughts, when I could focus once more, Caleb was singing...

Caleb's voice was so flat. His performance was...wooden. Where was *my* Caleb? Where was he, the brilliant actor who had stolen my heart? It was a rough start only, but...no. Caleb didn't warm to the role. I glance to my side. Seth and Daulton shifted uncomfortably in their seats.

As the play dragged on and on it grew worse if anything. The supporting actors did a fine job and managed to salvage much of the show, but Caleb... He was...dreadful. I was mortified. Why had I brought Seth and Daulton? I was completely and utterly humiliated. It was all I could do not to stand up and leave. I struggled to keep from crying.

We stood at the intermission and walked into the lobby with the crowd. I kept walking out the front doors. Seth and Daulton followed me.

"I'm so sorry for dragging you here tonight. I don't understand..."

"It's just a rough first night," Daulton said. "It happens to even the best of actors. Perhaps he is ill or received some bad news."

"Cheer up my boy, it isn't that bad," Seth said. "I will say he's very handsome—not as handsome as you, of course, but that is an impossibility. Perhaps his second performance will be better."

"I'm quite sure it will," Daulton said.

My friends were being kind and trying to comfort me, but it did not alter the truth. Caleb's performance was horrible. I was so humiliated I could barely look my friends in the eye.

"I can't watch anymore. I'm not going back in," I said. "Please do not feel you must stay on my account. Can I give you a rain check on supper? I need to be alone."

"Of course, dear Dorian," Daulton said. "Remember, I'm here for you if you need me."

Seth nodded.

"Have a good night, Dorian," Seth said.

I walked away so that my friends could leave without any feeling of having abandoned me.

"I told you," I heard Seth say to Daulton just before I passed out of earshot. "I told you that all romance ends in tragedy."

I could hear no more after that. I did not need to hear. Hot tears ran down my face. How could Caleb have been so horrible? He had been absolutely brilliant in class! He was, without question, the finest actor I had ever watched perform. What happened? It was as if someone else had come along and replaced the Caleb who had stolen my heart. Whoever it was upon that stage, he was *not* my Caleb. Everything was ruined.

I walked around campus trying to make sense of what had happened, but I could make no sense of it. Every possible explanation did not hold against rational thought. Caleb's performance had been terrible. There was no getting around that. He simply could not perform on stage in front of a large audience. There was no future for him in acting. I could have done a better job tonight. I was bitterly disappointed in him.

I lingered near the auditorium and when the crowds began to exit the doors I drew near. When most of the crowd was gone, I went in and found my way backstage. I asked about Caleb and was directed to a small dressing room.

When Caleb saw me he smiled.

"How badly I acted tonight," Caleb said, still grinning.

"It was dreadful. Are you ill? You have no idea how I've suffered tonight, on this night that was supposed to be so wonderful."

"Don't you understand, Dorian?"

"Understand what?"

"Why I was so bad tonight. Why I shall always be bad. Why I shall never act again."

"My only guess is that you are ill. You bored my friends tonight and me. I was humiliated in front of them."

Caleb seemed not to hear a word I said. He kept smiling!

"Before I met you, acting was the one reality of my life. It was only through the theater that I lived. When I played a part, I wasn't acting. I was that character. The painted scenery was my world. I thought it was all real, but you showed me it is not. Tonight, for the first time, I saw through the hollowness, the lie, the emptiness of it all. You made me understand what love really is! At first I did not understand what had happened to me, but as I stood upon the stage singing it all came to me. Theater is nothing. I'm tired of mimicking emotions. I have experienced real love, real emotion. I cannot act anymore."

I couldn't stand his ridiculous cheerfulness a moment more. I wanted to strike him.

"You have killed my love," I muttered, turning away.

Caleb put his hand upon my shoulder, but I shrugged it off. I turned back to him.

"Yes! You have killed it! You used to stir my imagination. Now you don't even stir my curiosity. I was in awe of your talent, but you've tossed it aside. You've thrown away a talent that others could only dream about it. You've lost it through foolishness. You are shallow and stupid! I was insane to have ever loved you. You are nothing to me now. I will never see you again. I will never think of you. I will never mention your name. I wish I had never laid eyes on you!"

"Dorian..."

Caleb tried to touch me but I shoved his hands away. I took off my ring and threw it on the floor.

"Dorian! I'm so sorry. Please! I love you!"

I turned my back on him and walked quickly out of the room. I hurried from the auditorium, fearful he would try to follow me. I lost myself on the forested paths to the south of the auditorium. I was stunned. Tonight was supposed to mark the beginning of Caleb's incredible career. Instead, it was the end. It was the end of us also. I hated him now. I hated myself for being stupid enough to love him.

I walked for hours, trying not to think about Caleb, but unable to think of anything else. How could everything have gone so utterly and so quickly wrong?

I returned to my suite exhausted. I downed a glass of wine and then fell onto the bed. Sweet oblivion took away all my sorrows, at least until I awakened the next morning.

When I opened my eyes the next morning I did not remember that my world had crashed into ruin. For a few brief moments I was happy. It was a bright and cheerful Saturday morning and Caleb and I...

That's as far as I got. It all came back to me. It feel upon me, weighting me down, as if the very sky was falling. I curled into a ball and cried.

I forced myself to get up. I thought of going out to breakfast, but I didn't feel like seeing anyone. The phone rang and I ignored it. Whoever it was could leave a message.

I found some Pop Tarts I didn't know I'd purchased and toasted them. I sat and ate while I tried to make sense of what had happened the night before.

I had not been kind. I had not listened when Caleb tried to explain. His words were only now coming through. They could not penetrate my pain, disappointment, and mortification the night before, but now...

Caleb had been a lonely boy before I'd met him. I knew that much from our conversations. Now, I understood he'd immersed himself in a fictional world until that world became real to him. It was no wonder he possessed such incredible acting abilities. He had stepped into roles not as an actor, but as the character himself. He didn't play Romeo. He was Romeo. He didn't play Tom Sawyer. He was Tom Sawyer. Meeting me and falling in love with me had pulled him into the real world. Caleb thought that meant he could no longer act, but he was wrong. Whatever made him such an excellent actor was inside him. It was a part of him. It could not go away.

I had to make him understand that and I would. Once I opened his eyes he would be a great actor again. I had said such horrible things to him that I wondered if he would see me now. I had told him I did not love him and that he was nothing to me. I had been cruel to him as I had been to no other. Something monstrous had broken loose in me, but I would rein it in. I would not let it control me.

I did love Caleb. I felt no love for him last night, but I had before and I did again now. I was foolish for thinking such a powerful emotion could just evaporate as if it had never existed. I did love him. The question now was would he forgive me? Did he still love me after I'd rejected him? I had to go to him and tell him how very sorry I was for everything. I had to do it soon. The longer I waited, the worse it would be, but I was afraid to go. What if he wouldn't forgive me? What if he told me he never wanted to see me again? My life would end then. I'd know I had thrown away happiness. I had to see him and I had to see him now.

Someone knocked on my door. I ignored it. They knocked more insistently. I angrily opened it.

"Seth?"

Seth never came to my dorm.

"I am so sorry, Dorian."

"What do you want?" I asked angrily.

"I know you may want to be alone, but I had to come check on you."

"I'm fine, Seth, absolutely fine. What happened last night was horrible, but I'm over it. I understand now."

"Dorian! Don't try to be brave. I know how much this must hurt you, must devastate you. I am so, so sorry."

I gazed at him confused.

"Come in," I said and closed the door once he'd entered.

"You sound as upset as I was last night. It was a dreadful performance. I must admit I was absolutely crushed and humiliated that Daulton and you were there to see it after I'd bragged so much about Caleb's superior acting abilities. I'm over it now, completely over it, or I soon will be. I spoke with Caleb after and said some horrible things I will not repeat to you, but I will set things right with him if I have to beg on my knees."

"You don't know," Seth said "Didn't you listen to my message? Haven't you read the paper?"

"What are you talking about?"

Seth stood there just staring at me with a look of pity on his face.

"Tell me!"

"Caleb is dead."

I just stood there staring at Seth. I felt as if I'd stepped out of reality. It couldn't be true, but Seth wouldn't lie. I knew I wasn't dreaming, but I also felt as if the world were suddenly unreal. I couldn't speak. I just stood there.

"I'm sorry to be the one to tell you this, but perhaps it's better than reading about in the paper. He killed himself last night."

"Suicide?" I managed to get out that one word of disbelief.

"Yes, the paper doesn't give any details, but I know someone in the police department. He gave me the particulars since the investigation has already been finished. It's a clear cut case of suicide. He left a note. It was vague, saying only that he couldn't go on and his life was no longer worth living, but it was a suicide note."

"How did he..."

"He hanged himself in his dressing room, not long after the performance apparently. The time of death is only an estimate, but he was found this morning."

I stumbled to the couch and dropped onto it, my head in my hands.

"I killed him."

"Dorian, he killed himself."

"I went to him after the play last night. I tracked him down in his dressing room. I said such horrible things, Seth. I told him I didn't love him. I threw my ring upon the floor. I left him in tears. I was probably the last person to see him alive. He killed himself because of me, Seth. I was going to seek him out this morning and set things right, but now..."

"You were on the road to disaster, Dorian. This is all for the best."

"How can you say that? Caleb is dead!"

"If he didn't kill himself and you set things right with him, you would have doomed both of you. Oh yes, I know. You've been living in a state of ecstasy because you loved Caleb, but it wasn't really ecstasy, it was delirium. The only possible outcome was tragedy. You would have tired of each other, irritated each other, and your love would have died, leaving you both bitter and resentful. That is the way love is, Dorian. It's a trap, as addictive and damaging as any drug."

"If you were so sure I was heading for disaster, why didn't you try to stop me?"

"You would not have listened, and as I've said before, all life ends in tragedy. There would have been joy along the way, but truly Dorian, this is for the best. You are free now and Caleb will become a romantic, tragic memory. You'll always remember him as the enchanting boy who was driven to despair by your beauty and love. You told me once you wanted your romance with Caleb to be theatrical. Your wish has been granted. What could be more theatrical than this?"

"Caleb is dead," I said.

"He has been spared the pain of living, Dorian. If we humans had any sense or courage we'd all kill ourselves on our thirtieth birthday at the latest, but we have neither sense or courage and therefore doom ourselves to decline and old age. Caleb will be young and beautiful forever and he'll be remembered, if not forever, at least for many long years and he will always be as he was on the night he took his own life. He did you both a favor, Dorian, and if you drove him to it you did both of you a great service. All his pain is ended and you are now free to enjoy your life."

"I meant to set things right. It's not my fault that I cannot."

"Exactly. You said you were responsible for Caleb's death. You couldn't be more wrong. No matter what you said to him, it was his choice. No one made him hang himself. He did it."

"He denied me the chance to make things right between us."

"You had good intentions, Dorian, but good intentions are nothing more than useless attempts to interfere with scientific laws. The result would have been pain and destruction for you both."

"I feel nothing now. Moments ago I felt grief and remorse, now I feel nothing. I feel as if I have been acting in a Greek tragedy and now that it is over I can walk away unscathed."

"Life's tragedies often wound us for their violence and lack of meaning, but this tragedy is a wonderful drama in which you were lucky enough to play a part. Caleb has killed himself for love of you. I wish that I had ever had such an experience. If those who love you stay too long in your life you cease to care about them, but Caleb has made himself immortal. You can always love him."

"You have made me feel much better, Seth. I think if you had not been here this morning...it would have been the beginning of a long depression and perhaps worse, but you have made me see the truth of the matter. I am lucky."

"Precisely. You have been given a great gift, Dorian, and now there is nothing that you, with your extraordinary good looks, will not be able to do."

"Thank you so much for coming, Seth."

"I have a special interest in you, Dorian. You are an extraordinary boy. I must be going, however, I have my own life to live."

I showed Seth to the door. When he had gone, my suite was silent. How odd it felt to know that Caleb was no more. He was there and then he was not. Seth was right. I could love him forever now and know that he died for love of me. I had accomplished my dream of an epic, theatrical romance and Caleb had possessed the good fortune to play a leading role. I had been right about him all along. He was destined to be a great actor. I had been wrong only about the stage upon which his performance would be set. I had pictured a Broadway theater or the big screen, but his stage had been Bloomington and I had walked upon it with him. He would forever be a star.

Chapter Eleven: The Picture of Dorian Gray

I walked into my study and gazed at my portrait. I froze in place for a moment. It was not possible, but the eyes had become hard and the lines of the lips cruel. The Dorian who gazed at me had a sense of menace and spitefulness to him. I had thought before that the portrait looked different, but I had dismissed the idea as ridiculous. Now, I was certain the painting had changed, but that wasn't possible. Was it? If only there was a way, but...yes! There was!

I walked to my desk and rummaged through the drawers. I pulled out an 8x10 print I'd had made for insurance purposes. I walked to the painting and held them side by side. There was no doubt I was correct. It was impossible, or rather I had thought it impossible, but my portrait had changed. There was no cruelty or malice emanating from the painting in the photo, but I felt as if the painting itself was gazing at me with baleful hatred. The portrait and the photo of the portrait should have been identical, but they were not. I walked to a mirror and held the photo up beside my reflection. The Dorian in the photo looked exactly as I did now.

I turned and stared at the painting again. Could it be? Was it really possible? I would not have thought so but for the obvious evidence before my eyes. I remembered my wish on the day my portrait was finished—that the painting would age in my place. My wish had come true, but there was deeper meaning to the wish than I had guessed. The events of our lives were written upon our features. Only now did I understood that as I saw the evidence before me. Every act of cruelty left its mark. Every ugly act was etched upon our features. Such ugliness would never mar my beauty. My wish had been granted. The deal had been closed. I knew with absolute certainty that my portrait would bear not only the ravages of time for me, but also my sins, for those sins were already evident on its features.

I grabbed a sheet and covered the portrait. I would order a thick, black, satin cover for it immediately, but the sheet would have to do for now. I could never allow anyone to see the portrait, especially Daulton and Seth for they would immediately notice the difference. No one would ever lay eyes upon the portrait, except me.

I left the study, closing and locking the door. I left my suite and walked out into the crisp November air. Winter was coming, but it would always be spring for me. I would never age. I would be young and beautiful forever. Seth had said that with my good looks I could do anything and he was right. The world was mine, not only for a few short years, but forever. I was immortal.

Today, my new life would truly begin. I stepped away from my old life with no regret. I had played at following Seth's philosophy, but now I would make it mine and live it. I would be all about pleasure and experience now. I would indulge my every desire.

I walked across campus and returned to the Runcible Spoon. I ordered myself another delicious Tex/Mex omelet. I could feel Caleb's ghost there with me, like the ghost of Hamlet's father, but he did not speak to me. He was my past. He had played his part and now he had walked off the stage.

It was almost too chilly to sit outside, but I'd had the foresight to wear a thick sweatshirt. I wasn't bothered by other diners. I sat there in peace and enjoyed my second breakfast. This one was much better than the Pop Tarts I'd eaten early in the morning. My life had changed so much since then and barely two hours had passed! Life was truly wonderful, for me at least.

After finishing off my omelet and a couple of cups of coffee, I walked the short distance to the square. I browsed in the bookstores and unique little shops. I also browsed the attractive young men, trying to decide which I wanted to take home with me. Two different girls did their best to get my attention, but I ignored them. They were of no use and of no interest to me.

As I was gazing in a window, I noticed the reflection of a handsome boy looking at me. He had no idea I could see him, but his eyes devoured me. He was a high school boy, his size, youthful face, and purple Bloomington South hoodie made that obvious. I guessed he was probably sixteen and a sophomore. Not a boy and yet not a man. He was only two years younger than me, but he possessed the look of pure innocence. He was probably yet to have his first sexual experience and he gazed at me with lust and longing.

I gazed at him while he gazed me. His hair was chocolate brown and his eyes dark. He was quite handsome.

I turned and caught him in the act. He quickly looked away and pretended to be interested in window shopping.

"I'm Dorian," I said.

"Oh, uh, hi. I'm uh...Trent."

Trent blushed. He was so cute.

"I'm getting a chill. Can I buy you a cup of hot cocoa? We can talk."

"Um...sure."

I knew I had perplexed him, just as I also knew he would follow me. He was nervous and likely frightened, but he desired me. That desire would override all fear, thought, and caution.

I led him down the street to the Scholar's Inn Bakehouse. I bought us both a hot cocoa and we found a quiet booth.

"Do you go to IU?" Trent asked, working up the courage to speak at last.

"Yes, I'm a freshman. You're in high school and go to Bloomington South."

Trent's mouth dropped open.

"How did you know that?"

"You're wearing a Bloomington South hoodie."

"Oh! Duh! Now I feel foolish."

I laughed and soon Trent was laughing with me.

"You're very cute, especially when you laugh," I said.

Trent blushed.

"And when you blush."

Trent turned a deeper shade of red.

"What are you doing today, Trent?"

"Nothing. I'm just hanging out."

"Saturdays are good for that. How would you like to come back to my dorm with me?"

Trent looked frightened for a moment, but even more excited.

"I'd like that a lot." His voice went husky with desire.

I reached across the table and ran my hand over his own for a moment and smiled at him. I would have bet a million bucks that Trent was hard as a rock at that moment.

We finished off our hot cocoa and I bought us a couple more to go. We strolled through downtown and onto campus. Trent nervously chatted away and asked a few questions. When he discovered I was a theater major he began to tell me all about his drama classes and the plays he had been in. Why was I not surprised he was a little drama queer?

A few minutes later, we walked into Read and I led Trent to my suite.

"Wow! I thought dorm rooms were supposed to be small?"

"Most are. This one is meant to be shared by three, but I have it all to myself. I've also made several improvements. It was quite tacky when I arrived."

"How did you manage getting this all to yourself?"

"I can do almost anything."

Trent looked at me with an expression of awe and admiration.

"Take off your sweatshirt. I keep it warm inside."

Trent pulled off his hoodie to reveal a slim body covered by a pink polo. He was very cute and sexy.

"How old are you, Trent?"

"I'm sixteen."

I nodded. I believed sixteen was legal in Indiana, but it didn't really matter. Only Trent and I would know what happened in my suite.

I stepped up to Trent. He gazed up at me. He was only about 5'9", some three inches shorter than me. I leaned down and kissed him. It was a brief kiss, but when it ended he was breathing much harder.

I pulled him to me and kissed him again, more deeply this time. I could feel his hardness pressing into me. I slid my tongue in his mouth and kissed him deeply. We made out for a few minutes. Trent was awkward at first, but he quickly mastered making out. When I pulled back he was nearly panting.

"I can't believe this is happening," he said. "You're the most incredibly looking guy I've ever seen. I can't believe…"

"Believe it," I said. "Are you a virgin?"

Trent nodded and blushed. I smiled. Damn, I loved virgins. There was something especially intense about leading a guy through his first time. I was determined to make sure Trent's first time was one he'd never forget.

I pulled off Trent's shirt, then mine. His torso was smooth and hairless, except for the faintest trail of dark hair leading into his jeans. He was slim, not muscular at all but his chest and abdomen was beautifully shaped. I reached out and ran my hand over his chest. His skin was perfectly smooth. His small nipples were erect. Trent hesitantly reached out and touched my chest, then began to run his hands all over me.

I led him to the bed and lay down on my back, allowing him to explore my body. He ran his hands all over my torso and then hesitantly kissed my chest. He extended his tongue and licked me. I put my hands behind my head and gave myself up to him.

When he licked my nipple, I moaned and pressed his head down. Trent took my cue and began to lick and suck. There was so much I could teach this boy, even though he was only two years younger. I hadn't been with that many guys myself, but I was experienced and I'd already learned so much.

I pulled Trent's face to mine and kissed him deeply again. I rolled him onto his back and explored his torso with my lips and tongue. I was more aggressive than Trent and he wiggled and squirmed with delight.

He breathed harder as I unfastened his belt, popped the button on his jeans, and pulled down the zipper. I pulled his jeans down and off, tossing them to the floor. I pulled his boxer-briefs down next and soon he was lying naked on my bed. I reached out and grasped him. He whimpered with pleasure

I leaned over Trent and enveloped him with my mouth. No sooner did my lips touch his cock than he exploded with a loud moan.

I pulled off when he'd finished and lay down beside him.

"I'm so embarrassed," he said.

"Don't be."

"I came in half a second. That's probably a world record."

"I don't know if Guinness keeps track of such things."

Trent's body shuddered and a sob escaped.

"Hey. Hey, it's okay. Really, it's nothing. This is your first time. Of course you're going to cum fast. Besides, there's plenty left where that came from."

I reached down and groped him. He was hard again in seconds.

Instead of speaking. I leaned over and went to work on him again. Soon, Trent was moaning and running his fingers through my hair. I went at it for a good ten minutes, then stopped. I wanted him all worked up for what I had planned.

I lay back. Trent stripped me naked with no hesitation. He licked my torso again and I pushed his head down. He followed my silent instruction and wrapped his lips around me. I moaned.

Trent wasn't good, but then he'd never given a blow-job before. Still, his lips felt deliciously soft, silky, and wet as they slid along my length.

"Teeth!" I hissed. "Cover your teeth."

Trent's technique improved as he figured out what worked and what didn't. He couldn't begin to swallow me, but I couldn't expect that from a virgin.

I ran my fingers through Trent's hair. I was getting worked up. I grasped the sides of his head and moved it up and down. I grew a little too aggressive and made him gag, so I eased off, then let him go at it himself. I was getting so worked up I couldn't wait anymore. I sat up and pulled away from Trent.

He lay back on the bed, leaning up on his elbows, watching me as I walked to the dresser and pulled out a bottle of lube. His eyes darted about fearfully as I put some lube into my hand and stroked myself.

"Dorian, I don't know if I can...I've never..."

"You want it, don't you?"

"I...I don't know."

"When will you get another chance? I'm sure it's hard to meet guys at your high school."

"More like impossible."

"How many of them look like me?" I asked, smiling.

"No one looks as good as you."

"So..."

Trent still hesitated. I gazed at him a few moments and then walked across the room towards my clothes.

"If you don't want to, I can take you home now..."

"No, wait."

I stopped.

"You'll go easy?"

"Of course," I said, smiling.

Trent swallowed hard and nodded.

I walked toward him.

"Shouldn't we use a condom?" he asked.

"You're a virgin, right? Or did you lie to me?"

"I've never even kissed a guy before this evening."

"I just got out of a relationship. It's safe."

"Okay," Trent naively agreed.

I should have used protection, but I wanted to feel myself in him bare. I wanted to seed him. It was like planting a flag on the top of Everest, proving that I was there first. Besides, he owed me. He owed me for bringing him home and allowing him to have sex with me.

"Lay on your stomach."

I climbed on top of Trent and firmly, but gently pushed. Nothing happened, but I kept trying. After several moments I slipped in and Trent cried out in pain.

"Take it easy. It only hurts at first and after you've done it once, the next time will be easier."

I went slowly. I wanted to get all the way inside him. I eased myself in. Trent tensed and whimpered, but I slowly inched myself in.

"I can't! Take it out!"

"Hold on. The worst is almost over. You don't want to miss out on the pleasure now that you've gone through most of the pain."

Trent groaned as I took him. His fists tightened on the pillows and he panted. I sank myself all the way into him and just lay there on top of him, reveling in the knowledge that I was the first to penetrate Trent's no longer virgin ass. No matter what happened now what I had done could not be undone. I grinned with satisfaction.

I began to slowly thrust in and out. I didn't go deep at first, but gradually I buried myself in further and further. Trent began to relax and even moan. He still whimpered and cried out in pain now and then, but I knew he was beginning to like it, even though it sometimes hurt. I was teaching Trent about the exotic sensuality of mixing pleasure and pain.

I began to take less care and concentrate more on what I wanted. Trent was just a toy after all. I'd use him this once and then perhaps never again. I had him where I wanted him and I intended to get all I wanted before he left.

I went at him harder, giving into instinct and primitive aggression. Trent tried to get up, but I held him down. I grabbed his wrists and held him in place. I had him pinned to the bed. He didn't actually tell me to stop. Perhaps he was afraid I wouldn't and he was right. I would not have stopped for anything.

I thrust into Trent, moaning and groaning. I used him. He was there for my use after all. His own pleasure was incidental. I thrust deeper and harder until I moaned and cried out in ecstasy. I claimed Trent as my own.

I rolled off Trent and he moved onto his back. He was crying, but his tears quickly stilled. I reached over, wrapped my fingers around him, and with a few strokes sent him into moaning ecstasy.

I got up and pulled on my clothes. Trent took the hint and got dressed too.

"Need a ride?" I asked. I believed in putting my toys away when I was finished with them.

"I think I'll walk. I have a lot of thinking to do."

"I bet you do," I said.

"Um, well...I guess I'll see you around."

"You might get lucky," I said and winked.

"Bye."

"Bye," I said.

I grabbed Trent's ass just as he left out the door. It was one last feel of what had been mine.

I took a shower, going over the events of the last couple of hours in my mind. I'd popped Trent's cherry. No matter how many times he hooked up or how many relationships he had I would always be his first. Nothing could change that or take it away from either of us. I had no doubt he was feeling used right now and I *had* used him. I'd intended to use him from the moment I set eyes on him. I had also taught him a lot and given him a lot in exchange. Trent knew he had been used, but he would remember me forever as the incredibly hot college boy who had picked him up and gave him his first sexual experience. I was also his first lesson in hookups. He'd likely be more cautious the next time a guy tried to pick him up.

As I climbed out of the shower and began to dry off I realized I'd completely forgotten about Caleb. At this time yesterday I was thinking about taking Daulton and Seth to see what I thought was the beginning of Caleb's brilliant career. How little did I know that Caleb would have no career, our relationship would go down in flames, and Caleb would kill himself. How little did I expect that I could rise from the flames like a phoenix and move on so easily. Caleb was already becoming no more than a bittersweet memory.

My phone rang. I had been expecting it. I was surprised it hadn't been ringing hours earlier. I knew before I picked it up that it was Daulton.

As soon as I picked up the receiver, Daulton filled my ear with condolences and concern for my well-being. When I was able to get a word in I assured him I was quite all right. I could not convince him. I sighed. I told him I would be at his studio in a few minutes to pick him up for lunch.

I was not looking forward to my afternoon as I set out in my Jag, but I began to change my mind as I neared Daulton's studio. I did enjoy spending time with him and I did so all too infrequently. Daulton and Seth were the closest thing I had to friends.

Poor Daulton. It was obvious he'd been crying when he came out of his studio and climbed into my Jag. He actually grabbed me and hugged me and I had to endure his, "Dorian, I am so very, very sorry." I didn't have the heart to tell him I'd completely forgotten about Caleb while I was pounding a high school boy only an hour before.

Daulton suggested the Irish Lion so I drove the short distance to the pub and parked on Kirkwood. We were shown to a small table upstairs which was at least semi-private. We ordered our drinks and browsed the menus. Daulton didn't say anything, but kept giving me sympathetic looks.

Daulton ordered Chicken Cordon Bleu and I ordered the Liffey Trout. Our waiter brought us a plate of soda bread to share. I had eaten in the Irish Lion before. I loved the atmosphere. I really felt as if I was inside an Irish Pub in the Victorian era. The soda bread was delicious.

"You must be devastated," Daulton said.

"Truthfully, no."

"You don't have to be brave, Dorian."

"I'm not being brave. His death came as a shock, certainly, and my world was shaken to its core, but I have adjusted to the reality of the situation. I can't change what happened and I can either wallow in grief or go on."

"Perhaps his loss hasn't truly hit you yet. Such things can take time."

"I'm well aware I will never see Caleb again. I had a future planned for us and now those plans lie in ruin. Last night's performance was...well, let's be honest, dreadful. I was terribly disappointed and upset about that, but this morning I realized it was an aberration. I knew the level of acting of which Caleb was capable and I was confident I could bring it out in him. Then, I received the news of his death and that changed everything."

I did not tell Daulton about my argument with Caleb, nor about the horrible things I'd said to him. I had hurt him horribly, but I was now convinced I was not responsible for his death. I may have driven him into despair, but it was Caleb who made the decision to end his life. I didn't force him. I didn't even suggest such a thing. If only he had held on he could have been sitting across the table from me instead of Daulton, but no, he gave up. There was no reason to give Daulton any details. I knew I could count on Seth's discretion. He alone would know the truth.

"If anything, I am angry with him," I said.

"Angry?"

"He was weak. He gave up. Instead of facing his problems and trying to go on he took the coward's way out."

"Isn't that a little harsh? Obviously he was in great pain."

"We all suffer great pain, Daulton, but most of us do not hang ourselves. He destroyed the life I had planned with him. He stole it from me and he stole himself from me. Yes, I am angry with him and I do not know if I will forgive him. So, pardon me if I shed no tears. Why should I grieve over someone who walked out on me? His pain is gone, but he has left me to struggle on."

"I expected to find you inconsolable," Daulton said.

"Would you have liked that better?"

"No, of course not. I am glad you are dealing with this so well and anger is one of the steps of grief. I do want you to know that I am here for you if you need me, Dorian."

"I appreciate that," I said with a smile. "I'm going to be fine, indeed I'm mostly fine now. I won't pretend Caleb's suicide has not affected me or that it will not affect me in the future, but unlike him I will not give up. I will go on. My life is too extraordinary not to live and I'm the only one who can live it."

"Well said."

"If you really want to help me, do not mention Caleb to me again. If I wish to talk about him, I promise I will contact you. I may well wish to speak of him in the future and if I do I know you are there for me."

"As you wish."

"Now, let's have a wonderful supper while you tell me about your latest projects. You know I'm very interested in your art."

Mercifully, Daulton made no further attempt to comfort me. I knew he meant well, but his sympathy annoyed me. As far as I was concerned, I had dispensed with the matter of Caleb. He was in the past and I lived in the present. He had made a choice and I had to live with it.

We talked until our meals arrived and then talked more. Daulton told me all about his latest pieces. My trout was excellent. I realized at that moment that it was difficult to find a bad meal in Bloomington. It was another reason to stay here. I would have to give some thought to my long term plans. I wasn't absolutely certain, but I believed that with my portrait aging for me I would live forever. If not, I'd likely live a very, very long time and that would take planning. I could not attend IU for decades without arousing suspicion. I smiled at that thought, but luckily Daulton believed it was in response to our conversation.

We lingered over dessert. Daulton did not return to the topic of Caleb, but I could sense him observing me to make sure I was handling the situation as well as I claimed. He was a good friend and I enjoyed spending the afternoon with him. I must admit I had not eagerly anticipated our time together, but once the subject of Caleb was dispensed with it had turned out to be a most enjoyable lunch.

I returned Daulton to his studio after we finished eating. Daulton and I said our goodbyes and I drove back to Read. I closed myself in my suite. I stared at the locked door to my study for a few moments, then walked over and unlocked the door. I entered the room and pulled the sheet off my portrait. The corners of Dorian's mouth were pulled up in a sneer. He was not as beautiful as he had once been. There was beauty in his features still, but that beauty had been marred by a look of disdain, smugness, and cruelty. I knew without a doubt that this is how I would have looked if I had never made my wish. How lucky I was to have made that wish! How lucky I was that Seth inspired it! How lucky I was to have met Daulton and how lucky he had created this doppelganger for me!

I covered my portrait again and once more locked the door. I slipped the key into my pocket, secure in the knowledge that only I would ever know the real Dorian Gray.

Chapter Twelve: A Much Needed Break

News of Caleb's suicide was all over campus. The Indiana Daily Student had featured an article about it, but even without the campus newspaper coverage, everyone would have known. I was able to avoid attention during the weekend by spending my time in art galleries, upscale restaurants, and other locations the majority of college students didn't frequent, but come Monday morning I had no choice but to attend classes. Well, I always had a choice, but I wished to continue at IU and so I couldn't skip. More than that, I wanted to attend. I just didn't want the attention that came from being associated with Caleb.

There were looks of sympathy from some students. Others told me how very sorry they were for my loss. Most students had no idea I even knew Caleb, but many had seen us together often enough to know we were friends. Some had seen us holding hands or kissing and knew we were more than friends. IU was a large school and yet it was a community. Everyone most definitely did not know everyone else and yet it was easy to be well-known if one stood out. My beauty and my Jag made me one of the few that most students recognized. At the moment, such notoriety was not desirable.

Acting for Theater Majors was my most difficult class of the day. Caleb and I had made no effort to hide our relationship and it was most obvious in our acting class. I was inundated with sympathetic looks as soon as I entered and several of my classmates expressed their sympathy or gave me a reassuring pat on the back. How callous they would have thought me had they known I was already over my grief when Caleb had not yet been buried!

Weston gazed at me sadly. He, more than any other, seemed to feel for me and that was significant for many members of our drama group were greatly concerned about me. I was annoyed by it and yet I appreciated it.

It look a few minutes to extricate myself from the well-meaning, compassionate drama queers after class ended. I was just making my escape when Weston stepped in beside me and walked with me down the hallway.

"I'm sure you're sick of talking about Caleb's death and don't even want to think about it anymore, so I'll only say I'm here for you if you need me," Weston said.

"Thank you."

"This is totally inappropriate I know, but...if you need some company..."

I looked at Weston. He was quite cute in an innocent way. I remembered the nights we had spent together.

"Things have been stressful. I know this football player...maybe I can arrange something for the three of us."

Weston looked like he'd just won the lottery. I nearly laughed.

"He does like to play rough. Think you can handle two tops?"

"To be with you *and* a football player, I'll do anything."

I smiled. Here was a boy I could use.

"Good. We may hold you to that. The next time Gabrial and I get together we may want a third."

"Gabrial? Gabrial, I'd sell my soul just to lick his chest, Diaddio? The quarterback?"

This time I did laugh.

"Yes. I'm sure I can trust your discretion."

"Of course! I've told no one about you...about what we've done."

"If you had we wouldn't be talking now," I said.

"I will do anything you guys want. *Anything*," Weston said. The sound of desperation in his voice was both pathetic and arousing. I wanted to take him to my suite and use him immediately, but it would take time to arrange things with Gabrial.

"I'll let you know."

Weston had another class so I was soon rid of him. I returned to Read and lost myself in schoolwork. I had more than one report due as well as a project. I dove into my work, mostly because it would keep my isolated from campus life. The unwanted attention I received as Caleb's friend and lover would soon die down. In a week, he'd be forgotten by most. The more I could stay out of public view the more undesirable sympathy I could avoid. I would use the time to do my schoolwork and to work ahead so that I could hit the parties and get back into campus life when I was no longer the center of attention. I enjoyed the attention I received because of my looks, but I did not like the Caleb-related attention at all. The sooner it was over, the better.

***

The week passed too slowly, but I hit a party on Friday night. Two aggressive girls were all over me, going so far as to grope my ass and feel me up. They interested me not at all, but any hand on my package felt good and it made some of the boys standing near burn with jealousy. *That* I enjoyed.

I thought about seducing another inebriated, straight, frat boy, but a rather sexy college boy was checking me out. He was a little buzzed, but far from drunk. He was obviously gay, at least it was obvious to me. I could read it in his eyes as he looked at me with lust. He was tall and slim with dark eyes and hair. He was good-looking if somewhat too thin. His lips were red and full. I smiled at him and he grinned back.

The party was in a rented house a couple of blocks south of campus. There were couples making out and groping here and there and everyone was drinking. I disentangled myself from the girls, gazed at my admirer for a few long moments, and then went in search of a semi-private place where I could make use of him.

There was a very small pantry off the kitchen with just enough room for two. I stepped in and looked back. The boy had followed as I knew he would. I gazed at him once more, stepped into the pantry, and waited until he joined me. Once he was in I closed and locked the door. I pushed him to his knees and leaned back against the door while he went to work. He was good. He was damned good. I could tell he'd done this often before.

After a few minutes, I grabbed him by the hair and pulled him to his feet. I stripped his jeans and boxers away, pushed his face against the door, and entered him. I wasn't gentle. I pushed myself deep inside him and grinned when he grunted. I thrust into him over and over. He let me use him. I kept at it for a few minutes and then I moaned loudly and shoved myself all the way in.

I pulled out, the boy turned around and fisted himself wildly until he too moaned. We pulled our pants up and left. A couple of guys looked at us, but with no special interest. No one really cared if a couple of guys fucked in a pantry, unless they were impatiently waiting to use it themselves.

I hadn't spoken a word to the boy. I didn't know his name. I doubted I'd ever see him again and I didn't care. We had both gotten what we wanted. I wanted to use him and he wanted to be used.

I went straight back to my dorm and feel asleep. Sex was better than a sleeping pill. It always put me right out.

***

I spent the holidays in London. I rented myself a flat and stayed there during the entire break. I enjoyed the anonymity, the museums, the art exhibits, the fine dining, and the clubs. There were also pretty British boys to bring back to my flat if I felt the need for companionship. I loved the UK boys and their accents. The boys were only a part of my holidays. There was far more to life than sex. Only those who don't get it obsess over sex, like the poor straight boys back at IU. I bet they didn't get it nearly as often as the gay guys. They didn't know what they were missing. I could find a guy to sate my lust anytime I desired, so sex wasn't an obsession for me. It was only one of many pleasures of my life.

I thought of Caleb as I walked around the theater district. He would have loved it if I'd brought him here. I would have done so had he not ended his life. Suicide truly was the ultimate in foolishness. I had been harsh and Caleb believed I didn't love him anymore. When he took his life it was possibly true that I did not love him at that moment, but if he had held on everything would have been set right. If he would have just stuck it out for a few more hours I would have patched things up between us. Caleb should have been held up as an example to those who contemplated suicide. His corpse should have been displayed on TV while a narrator informed the audience that the lifeless body had once been a boy who could have had everything, if only he hadn't let anguish overwhelm him. What a stupid, stupid boy.

I didn't have to worry about suicide, of course. I would never feel like ending it all. The world was mine and would be, if not forever, then for a very long time. All thanks to a portrait that was safely locked away in storage hundreds of miles away enshrouded in black satin. No, I would never make Caleb's mistake. I could do anything my heart desired.

Christmas in London was wonderful. Gavin, a friend I'd made by chance in an art gallery, invited me to spend Christmas day with his family. He assured me many would be dropping in so I needn't feel out of place. I accepted his offer out of curiosity.

Gavin was a year older than me, quite handsome, and interested in art. He'd taken me to many places I would have missed without him. He'd lived in London all his life, so he knew the city well. London was one of the largest cities in the world, but it seemed more like a grouping of small towns to me.

Gavin's family lived in a large, elegant townhouse. Back home we would have considered the Georgian structure quite old, but here a structure built in the eighteenth century attracted no special attention.

I was welcomed at the door and ushered into a very well appointed foyer. Gavin spotted me and led me into a parlor where the main festivities were taking place. He introduced me around, but I couldn't begin to remember all the names. There was a large, old-fashioned Christmas tree all decked out in lights and antique ornaments. I stood and gazed at it long in fascination. There was so much beauty in the world for those who took the time to notice it.

We celebrated the holiday with a formal, but in no way stuffy, dinner that included roast goose and a Christmas pudding among other things. The pudding was not a pudding at all, but more like a cake. After dinner, crackers were passed around. Not crackers as in saltines, but small tubes wrapped in pretty Christmas paper that banged when pulled apart. Inside were little prizes like funny hats and trinkets. A rather potent Christmas punch was liberally dispensed and it made the party very merry. This was definitely much more fun than the quiet Christmas I'd planned in my flat. I almost felt as if I was inside a Dickens Christmas story.

Gavin was quite handsome, but his younger brother, Maxxie, was extraordinary. He possessed the same wavy black hair and enchanting blue eyes, but he oozed sensuality. I guess he was a year or two younger than me. He had the same slim built of his brother and I guessed that he was defined. Our eyes kept meeting over dinner and during the later festivities too. I thought of Gavin as a friend, but I decided quickly that I would have Maxxie before I departed.

The seduction of the boy was not difficult. With a few smiles I was able to determine he wanted me. I signaled with my eyes that I wanted to be alone with him. Maxxie gazed around secretively, the motioned with his head for me to follow him. We slipped out of the room, down a short hall, and then up the stairs. Maxxie pulled me into a room, closed the door, and turned on the light.

There was no doubt the room was his. There was a single bed of mahogany and a matching dresser that looked as if they might be as old as the townhouse. The rest of the room screamed "teen boy." There were posters of soccer players, a soccer ball, and a soccer trophy. I had no doubt Maxxie was a soccer player, which I believed was called football in the UK. Maxxie's athletic prowess made me want him even more.

We could not absent ourselves from the party long so I pulled Maxxie to me and kissed him deeply. He responded immediately. I unbuttoned his shirt and ran my hands over his smooth and slim, but muscled and defined chest. We stripped off our shirts as we made out, then loosened belts, popped buttons, and pulled down zippers. Maxxie lowered his head to my chest and begin to lick and suck my nipples.

Maxxie returned to my lips soon. We made out while our hands explored. I traveled down his torso, mimicking his earlier moves, but then sank to my knees and pulled him into my mouth. Maxxie moaned with passion.

I worked my young lover into writhing ecstasy, then traveled slowly back up his smooth body. Maxxie wasted no time in dropping to his knees before me. His expertise left no doubt that I was not the first he had served.

The minutes were slipping by much too quickly. As reluctant as I was to stop Maxxie, there was something I wanted more. I pulled him to his feet, then walked him over to his desk with some difficulty as we had not taken off our shoes or socks and our pants were gathered around our ankles. Maxxie leaned on his desk while I positioned myself behind him. He groaned as I slowly entered him.

I do not think I was the first to enter Maxxie. He took it too easily. He grunted and whimpered in pain only a very little. Mostly, he moaned and breathed harder in his excitement. Within moments I was pumping away, enjoying yet one more pleasure that England had to offer.

I was so consumed with thrusting myself deeply into Maxxie that I was not aware his bedroom door had opened until I heard a gasp. I turned to see Gavin staring at us, his mouth dropped open in surprise. Maxxie gasped as well and stood up. I pushed him back down with one hand while I motioned his brother into the room with both my eyes and head. Gavin hesitated for a long moment, then stepped in and closed the door behind him.

Gavin moved forward awkwardly, but I beckoned him forward with my eyes even as I once again began to thrust into his younger brother. Gavin leaned in and kissed me upon the lips. I deepened the kiss and soon our tongues were entwined. I knew then that I had him

"Take off your clothes," I said quietly when we broke our kiss.

Gavin complied. I was struck by the similarity of Gavin and Maxxie's builds. Maxxie was somewhat more muscular, but otherwise was a slightly shorter version of his brother. Maxxie was definitely more beautiful, but Gavin had received his share of the family good looks.

Gavin and I kissed some more as I continued to pump into his little brother. I had always wanted to be with brothers and now my wish had come true.

I withdrew from Maxxie and guided Gavin toward him. There was some reluctance, but Gavin's lust overwhelmed him and he took my place behind Maxxie and entered him. Maxxie moaned.

I stepped behind Gavin and pressed myself against him, determined to discover if I could slip inside the older sibling as easily as I had the younger.

Gavin cried out in pain as I entered him. My question was answered. Maxxie was not a virgin, but Gavin's cherry had not been popped... until just then. I took it easy and slowly pressed myself into him even as I felt him thrusting into his little brother. I smiled with the depravity of it all. Oh! The things I could make boys do—things they would have never done had I not seduced them!

Quiet moans, whimpers, and groans filled Maxxie's bedroom. I drank in the sight of Gavin on Maxxie even as I used Gavin for my pleasure.

I began to breathe harder and thrust more urgently. The scene that was playing out was too hot. I moaned loudly and seeded Gavin. Only moments later he moaned too, and I knew he was breeding his younger brother.

Gavin and I did not forget about Maxxie after our orgasms. Maxxie turned around and I pulled Gavin onto his knees with me. With both leaned in and took turns giving pleasure to Maxxie, who panted and moaned. Gavin's lips were around Maxxie when his little brother lost control. I watched in fascination as Maxxie's orgasm ripped through his young body.

As soon as Maxxie was finished, we all stood and quickly dressed. The brothers would not look at each other. I smiled wondering how they would deal with what had happened here today. Would they continue with an incestuous relationship or try to pretend it had never happened? No matter what they did, nothing could undo what I'd done here today. I had seduced brothers into having sex with each other. I was entirely satisfied and that's all that mattered.

The three of us walked downstairs. I thanked Gavin and Maxxie's parents for their hospitality, which had been more wonderful than they could ever know. Gavin and Maxxie blushed and awkwardly looked away from each other as I bid them a Merry Christmas.

My days in London were too short and all too soon I was on a plane back to the states. I spent a couple of days in New York City and then flew to Indianapolis where I took the shuttle to Bloomington. Despite my wonderful holiday in London, it was good to be back.

Chapter Thirteen:
Sinking Deeper into Depravity

Spring Semester 1982

When I returned after the Christmas break most of the students had all but forgotten about Caleb. It was a new semester, with new classes. Some of the drama crowd were in my theater-related classes, but most were not. As a freshman, most of my courses were general and not involved with theater at all. I looked forward to my later years when I could focus on what truly interested me.

Weston shared my history of theater course which met on Monday, Wednesday, and Friday. We weren't friends, but we did begin sitting by each other. During our first Wednesday session, I leaned over before class started and whispered to Weston.

"We're on with Gabrial Sunday night if you're still interested."

Weston looked confused for a moment. It had been a few weeks since we'd discussed a possible thee-way. His confusion was short-lived.

"Really? Awesome!"

"Just remember your promise. You said you'd do *anything*."

A nervous and frightened expression crossed Weston's innocent features. I wondered if he'd back out, but the hungry look in his eyes made me hopeful. I could almost see lust and fear warring within him.

Weston nodded.

"I'll give you the details after class," I said, because the professor was about to begin.

Weston was by my side instantly the moment class ended.

"So...when? Where?"

"My dorm room. Sunday at 7 p.m. I'm working out with Gabrial at the SRSC and then we're going back to my place."

"You work out? I didn't figure you for the athletic type."

"I just started and I'm not athletic. I hate to sweat. I just want to add on a little muscle, not much, just a little size and definition."

"Good, if you started looking like a jock it would ruin your look. You're perfect as you are."

I grinned.

"I'm just making a minor adjustment, nothing big. I want more strength than anything. It's hard to fight some of these girls off."

Weston eyed me, trying to figure out if I was kidding or not. Actually, I wasn't. Some girls got *very* aggressive. I also thought it wise to have a little strength to use against jealous boyfriends. If Weston was worried I was going to try to get buff he could rest easy. I had no intention of dedicating any serious amount of time to working out.

"Gabrial and I discussed hooking up with you. Your promise that you would do anything we wanted convinced him."

"About that..."

"You're not getting scared, are you?"

"I...uh...well...I'm not all that experienced. I've gone further with you than anyone. I wouldn't have gone that far, but...I wanted you so bad."

"If you aren't willing to keep your end of the deal, don't bother showing up," I said.

Weston turned and looked at me. I wasn't smiling.

"You guys aren't going to hurt me, are you?"

"We're not going to do anything that will permanently damage you. It's sex, not a beating. Gabrial and I haven't mapped everything out. It will be mostly spontaneous. I'm sure there will be pain involved, but also pleasure. You just have to ask yourself if having sex with us is worth it. No one has ever been with the two of us before and maybe no one ever will be again. We're not going to try to hurt you, but we're also not going to care too much if what we do to you hurts. If you have the balls to show up, you'll be in for the most intense sexual experience of your life. If you don't...well, there won't be a second chance."

"I want to be with the two of you bad.   Either one of you alone...damn, but together? Wow."

"Just remember. If you want us, you have to pay the price. If you're not willing to pay the price, don't show up. We're doing this our way, or not at all."

Weston nodded. He didn't agree or disagree. I could read the conflicting emotions as they played across his face. Fear and lust raged against each other, but nervousness, suspicion, eagerness and a mass of other feelings also joined the fray. I doubted if even Weston would know if he was showing up or not until the moment came. He would be tormented by possibilities until Sunday evening. I must admit I derived a sadistic pleasure from watching him battle himself.

I wondered if Weston knew what he was getting himself into. He hadn't fussed when I'd been rough with him, but Sunday evening was going to be rougher. My own plans for Weston went beyond what I'd done with him before and I didn't know what Gabrial had planned. I doubted most guys could handle being gang-banged by two horny college boys, especially when one of them was hung. I wasn't ashamed of what I had, but Gabrial was *big*. I figured there was an even chance that Weston wouldn't show. His fear might well get the best of him. Then again, lust was a powerful force. I could but wait and see. If he failed to show Gabrial and I would have an intense sexual experience alone, but I must admit I hoped Weston would submit to us.

I spent most of my week attending classes, doing school work, and dining out. I picked up a cute boy in the SRSC on Friday and took him out to eat, then back to my place for some one-on-one action. He was my age, but shorter and more buff. He looked like a buff, tough wrestler, but he was all bottom in bed. I didn't mind at all. I liked to bottom, but there was something extra hot about topping a buff boy who could have snapped me like a twig. We both got off and he left happy.

A chill wind swept over the campus on Saturday morning and a steady snow-fall followed in its wake. It was a light snow, with tiny flakes. The kind that can fall for hours. The view from my windows was so enchanting that I bundled up in a black pea coat and my purple scarf and headed out into the winter wonderland.

I first headed east and walked past Forest Quad. I spotted Brendan, the buff football player I'd lusted after, taking off with two girls in a pink VW. Gabrial had warned me off Brendan. I didn't mind that Brendan had a boyfriend back home. Guys with boyfriends or girlfriends were a special challenge I enjoyed. I didn't make any moves because Gabrial and Brendan had become friends. Gabrial hadn't flat-out asked me to leave Brendan alone, but he was protective and obviously wanted him for himself. I smiled with the thought that the three of us might be hooking up for our own three-way by the end of the semester. I would have given a good deal to see Brendan naked.

I changed directions, walked back past Read, across Jordan Avenue and then through campus. I strolled up Kirkwood, past Nick's English Hut and on to the square. I stopped at the Scholar's Inn Bakehouse for a cup of hot cocoa and to warm up.

Two girls eyed me as I sat alone. It was really too bad I wasn't bi. I was missing out on a lot of sexual experiences. I could not will myself to be sexually attracted to females and the thought of sex with them was not appealing. I wouldn't mind one watching as I did her boyfriend, but I didn't so much as want to see one naked.

The girls walked over and I let them join me. I didn't mind their company. They were both fairly attractive, with nice bodies, dark hair, and attractive features. Their physical appearance didn't really matter to me as I had no physical interest in them.

We chatted. They flirted. I flirted back a little, but not much. I didn't want the hassle of ridding myself of them if they thought I was seriously interested. They were disappointed when I stood and told them I had to go, but luckily didn't ask for my number or try to give me theirs. I wouldn't have minded hanging out with girls a bit more if most of them weren't so predatory. Guys had a reputation for being sexual predators, but from what I'd experienced girls were just as ready to pounce.

As much as I loved summer warmth, I also loved the snow. It steadily drifted down all around me, beautifying the world. The cold did not bother me. I had once hated cold, but I saw it now as yet another sensation to explore. I yearned for new experiences and intended to indulge in as many as I could. Some such experiences fell on me out of the sky. Others had to be planned. I thought of Sunday evening and wondered if Weston would show. If not, Gabrial and I could surely find another boy to use soon enough. There were many guys on campus who would practically sell their soul to be with us. Some of them no doubt *would* sell their soul if that's what it took.

I loved anticipation. While I enjoyed spontaneous pleasurable experiences, I thrilled to those I could anticipate with eagerness. I liked to ponder the unknown. The possible three-way with Gabrial and Weston on Sunday evening was the perfect event to anticipate with eagerness. Not knowing if it would go down at all added a slight thrill. Wondering just what would happen was an even bigger thrill. I had some plans in mind, but a situation like that was fluid. I'd be playing off the actions and reactions of two other young men. Some things were not in doubt. Gabrial and I would dominate and use Weston. The possible details were endless. Should we seek to make the experience pleasurable for Weston so he would be willing to be our toy whenever we desired? Should we use him with no thought to him whatsoever knowing he was easy to replace? Just how far should we go? There were so many questions to ponder, so many possibilities!

I absolutely had to force myself to study on Saturday afternoon. I intended to hit a party that night and I doubted I could keep my mind on my books on Sunday. I lived to indulge and experience, but I was capable of long term goals, such as experiencing the world of theater to the fullest. I intended to leave IU not only with a degree, but also with a great deal of knowledge about a world I loved. Besides, time was no longer my enemy. There would be endless years for parties and sexy boys.

I slept in on Sunday morning. The party the night before had been wild and I'd drunk more than I should. I lingered in bed mostly because I wanted the time between the present and 7 p.m. to evaporate as quickly as possible.

What little remained of the morning passed quickly enough and I kept myself occupied with running around town, eating lunch at Bucceto's, and cruising College Mall. I bought myself a few shirts and some boxer-briefs in Abercrombie & Fitch. I pondered a new coat in Macy's, but I truly had no need of one. I sometimes wondered if those who couldn't instantly gratify their every desire might not have it better in a way. Wanting and not getting could create an enjoyable anticipation. Of course, those who could not afford what they wished would likely have slapped me in the face for such thoughts, but what did I really care?

At five, Gabrial picked me up in his cherry red Trans Am and drove me to the SRSC. There, I entered a part of his world, filled with weight machines and dumbbells, workout mats and...some things I couldn't even name. The weight room oozed masculinity, although girls worked out there too. Gabrial worked out shirtless and I loved to watch the girls, and some of the guys, drool over him. Even guys who were not sexually attracted to other males drooled over Gabrial. They wanted to look like him so bad they couldn't stand it. I nearly laughed out loud thinking about it. How pathetic.

As Gabrial hit his routine hard, I did my bench presses, lats, and other exercises at a more leisurely pace. I was quite sure Gabrial put in twice the workout I did. He was ten times more concerned about being buff than me so I think I was quite dedicated.

I enjoyed my proximity to Gabrial's mostly nude, flexing body. I enjoyed watching others drool over him. Gabrial gave me pointers from time to time. We talked between sets. It was obvious we were there together. Did anyone wonder about us? Did they suspect we fucked?

We showered after. Gabrial was a magnificent sight naked, but I caught him checking me out more than once. The look in his eyes told me how badly he wanted me. I didn't have his body, but then he didn't have my beauty. We weren't what I'd call opposites, not at all, but we had quite different body types. I loved to explore his hard, bulging muscles and Gabrial loved to run his fingers and tongue all over my smooth, slim form. This evening we would do that and much, much more.

"You think he'll show?" Gabrial asked as we climbed back in his Trans Am for the drive to Read.

"I'm thinking even chance. He wants us bad, but he's scared."

"He should be." Gabrial laughed.

I grinned. I loved Gabrial's wicked side.

We were soon back at Read. It was only a few minutes before seven so we wouldn't have to wait long to see if this was to be one-on-one or a three-way.

Gabrial and I sat close together on the couch. The air was filled with sexual tension and expectation. Gabrial leaned in and kissed me. We began to make out aggressively. I liked things rough. I had been disappointed in some boys because they were so tentative and calm. Sex was about arousal and aggression. It was about satisfying lusts and desires. It was meant to be intense and Gabrial was the perfect partner.

We were hot and heavy into making out when there was a knock at the door. I grinned, disentangled myself from Gabrial, and walked across the room. I opened the door. Weston stood there looking nervous and pale. There was a large bulge in the front of his corduroys.

"I'm here," he said.

"Are you sure you want to enter?" I asked. "Once you do there is no turning back until we're through with you."

Weston hesitated for a moment, then walked inside. I closed and locked the door.

"Scared?" Gabrial asked.

Weston nodded.

"You should be."

Weston's eyes grew a little wider and I knew he was wondering what he'd gotten himself into.

Gabrial pulled his shirt off.

"Holy shit!" Weston said, gawking at him.

"Let's see what you've got, freshman."

Weston pulled off his shirt, exposing his slim, but smooth, firm, and compact body.

"A little puny, but not bad," Gabrial said.

Weston blushed.

"Come here," Gabrial ordered.

Weston approached. Gabrial grabbed the back of his head and shoved Weston's face into his left pec.

"Start licking."

Weston was all over him and it wasn't because he was afraid of the consequences if he refused. I had the feeling he'd fantasized about something very much like this for a long time.

In the end it didn't matter. He'd given up his right to say no when he stepped in the door.

I stripped off my shirt, walked over, and worked on getting Weston naked while he worshipped Gabrial's chest with his tongue. Weston was stiff as a poker and it was hard getting his boxers down. I stripped naked, too, and pressed myself against him. I pulled his lips away from Gabrial's chest and shoved my tongue in his mouth.

Gabrial and I passed Weston back as forth, kissing him like he'd never been kissed before. Weston panted with excitement. Gabrial and I were getting worked up too. It was always hot between us, but this was even hotter.

Gabrial stepped back and stripped. Weston stared with an open mouth. I almost laughed. The sight of Gabrial naked was overwhelming. He was one of the few guys who could steal attention away from me. He was a young god.

Gabrial and I both grabbed one of Weston's shoulders and forced him to his knees. I shoved myself in his mouth.

"Get to work," I said.

I already knew Weston was good, but he seemed even more talented now. After just a couple of minutes, I pushed him off. Gabrial grabbed him and shoved himself in Weston's mouth. We passed him back and forth again. I was quite certain at this point that Weston had no desire to leave. I wondered how long he would feel that way.

I was feeling increasingly aggressive. I grabbed the sides of Weston's head and shoved myself in and out of his mouth. He gagged a couple of times, but didn't fight it. I made it clear through my actions I was intentionally using him. I wanted him to understand that he was my toy.

Gabrial took his turn using Weston next and his larger tool gave Weston more trouble. He tried to back off when he couldn't take it, but Gabrial just forced his head down. When we pushed Weston away, the boy was gasping for breath, but looking totally turned on by being used hard.

Gabrial and I decided to torment him by making him watch us. We stood there, made out, and ran our hands over each other's bodies while Weston looked on. I glanced at him once and I could tell he was eager to join in, but knew better than to do so without being given permission. The boy knew his place. He knew he was *very* lucky to be there.

Gabrial and I had discussed it and agreed that I'd take Weston from behind first. While I wasn't small, I was smaller than Gabrial. We weren't too worried about whether it hurt him or not, but we didn't want to use Weston so hard he'd never come back. While using him so severely he ran away screaming held some appeal, having access to him whenever we pleased had more value.

We grabbed Weston and forced him on his hands and knees. I grabbed a bottle of lube and prepared Weston and myself. I kneeled down behind him and took him with one long, slow thrust. He cried out and Gabrial silenced him by shoving himself into Weston's mouth. We spit-roasted our little boy toy.

Gabrial and I spent most of an hour switching positions, using Weston for our pleasure. A look of pain sometimes crossed Weston's cute face, but he spent most of his time moaning.

I'd exhibited excellent control, but after nearly an hour I just couldn't hold back anymore. I groaned, lay against Weston's back, and cut loose. That sent Gabrial over the top. He buried himself in Weston's mouth and moaned loudly. I watched his muscles tense and flex as his orgasm spread throughout his body.

Gabrial and I pulled out of Weston, sweat covered our bodies in a soft sheen. I didn't like to sweat, but I made an exception for sex. It was more than worth it.

Weston rolled over onto his back. There were tears in his eyes, but he was hard as a rock. He started to touch himself.

"We didn't give you permission to touch yourself," Gabrial said.

Weston quickly moved his hand away, but I could tell he was in desperate need. I just watched him for a few moments, enjoying his torment. I picked up his clothes and threw them at him.

"We're done with you. Get dressed and get out. I'll let you know if we want you again," I said.

Weston swallowed hard and almost looked like he was going to cry, but did as he was told. I noted with satisfaction that he moved awkwardly as he walked toward the door, although that was probably more Gabrial's doing than mine. Weston left.

"We really are bastards," Gabrial said.

"And your point would be?"

We both laughed.

"Damn. You're heartless, Dorian."

"Weston just had *the* sexual experience of his life. Yeah, we sent him away limping and nearly in tears. We humiliated and used him, but he knew we were going to do it and he still showed up. It was his choice. I really don't care if he liked it or not, but I bet he'll be remembering and fantasizing about this night for years."

"I'm not sure I'd want to meet you in a dark alley, Dorian," Gabrial said with a grin.

"You would be safe and so would Weston. This wasn't force. He submitted. I must admit that I'm going to enjoy looking him in the eye from now on. I'll bet you ten-to-one he blushes and looks away."

"I'd take that bet, but I don't like to lose."

We dressed and Gabrial stayed a while for cappuccino.

"It's too bad we can't invite your teammate over for a three-way," I said as Gabrial took a sip.

"I assume you mean Brendan. He would never be submissive like Weston."

"I was thinking more along the lines of an equal partner, not a submissive toy."

"You can forget any kind of three-way with him. He's hopeless devoted to his little boyfriend."

"And yet you'll seduce him."

"That was the plan, but..."

"There's a but? You're going to let someone you want slip away? That's not the Gabrial I know."

"I already let him escape."

"What?"

"Brendan became too good of a friend to seduce and use. I could have had him. He was weakening and ready to break, but..."

"If you're going to talk about a selfless act I don't want to hear about it, especially from you. It might weaken my admiration for you."

"Hey, there's an exception to every rule. If it will make you feel better I'll tell Weston he was a lousy fuck."

I laughed.

"I think you moaned too much to make *that* believable."

"Besides, letting Brendan go was not a selfless act. If anything, it was a selfish act."

"How so?"

"I valued him too much as a friend to throw what we had away for sex. I can get sex any time I want it, but Brendan...he breathes football as I do. We are two of a kind. Had I seduced him, he would have hated me for it after. I would have lost everything I had with him."

"I suppose your reputation is intact."

Gabrial laughed.

"Damn, I think I'm going to have to go home and go to bed. Sex relaxes me so much I get sleepy."

"You must be sleepy a lot then."

"You have no idea. Thanks for a great night, Dorian. Next time I'll supply the boy toy or we can just use Weston again."

"I think we should make him wait a while. I want to see how long it takes him to start begging for it."

Gabrial grinned and shook his head.

"Damn, I like you! You're even more wicked than me."

"You have no idea," I said, repeating his words.

Gabrial departed. I took a shower, then unlocked my study. I turned on the light and took the black satin cover off my portrait. I recoiled for a moment. The features of Dorian's face had grown lecherous, smug, and cruel. I experienced momentary regret at how I'd used Weston, but the sensation was fleeting. He knew what he was getting into. If it wasn't all he'd imagined that was his problem, not mine.

I walked to a mirror and gazed at myself. I was nearly amazed at my own beauty. I smiled. This was the real me.

I quickly covered up the portrait, turned off the light, and locked the door once more. I climbed into bed. Gabrial was right. Sex was relaxing. I closed my eyes and was sleeping peacefully in moments.

28 Years Later...

Chapter Fourteen: Dorian Becomes a College Boy...Again

Bloomington, Indiana
Saturday, August, 21 2010

I strolled along Kirkwood Avenue toward the Sample Gates, enjoying the early nighttime sights. The fall semester was about to begin and Kirkwood overflowed with students. I had lived in Bloomington for nearly thirty years now. It had been twenty years since I finished my graduate degree. Finally, I was returning to IU as a student once more.

I could have returned after ten years perhaps. All my fellow students and those likely to recognize me, with the exception of a few professors, would have been long gone. I waited a few more years to be extra cautious. As crazy as the idea would seem to my former classmates and professors, I didn't want anyone to have the least suspicion that I was I was same Dorian who had entered IU in the fall of 1982. If any professor did notice my uncanny resemblance to a student in their past, I would tell them I was Dorian Gray, II. I would pose as my own son.

I smiled. I was a freshman again. I was eager to get back into the thick of campus life. The proximity of my downtown apartment to campus had given me easy access to college boys throughout the years, but there was nothing like being an insider. It made the hunt that much easier. Besides, I enjoyed playing the part of a college boy. I had learned a great deal about acting in my eight years at I.U. After completing my B.A. I'd stayed on for an M.A. Why not? I had all the time in the world. This time around, I would study something different...

I crossed over Indiana Avenue and walked between the Sample Gates, the entrance to the Old Crescent area of IU. The gates had not even been built yet when I was a freshman the first time around, but then much had been added to the campus since that time.

The Old Crescent was my favorite part of campus. The oldest buildings were here, tall, stately, and elegant. I turned into Dunn's Woods. I loved to walk through the small forest, although it was nearly too dark to see at this time of night. Still, the paths were paved with brick and some light broke through from the street lights that lit most of the campus. There were even a few lampposts within the forest itself.

The woods were quiet and peaceful. Only an echo of the traffic on nearly Indiana Avenue disturbed the sounds of nature. All the rowdy college boys at Kilroy's on Kirkwood could not be heard at all. It was hard to believe that so much activity was so close to this tranquil place. I had walked in Dunn's Woods countless times over the years and yet I was always surprised when I stepped out to be faced by busy Indiana and Kirkwood Avenues.

I heard footsteps behind me, but didn't bother to turn. Many students walked here and couples came here to get intimate. Still, as I walked on and the footsteps continued to pace me I felt the hair on the back of my neck stand on end. There was a street light not far ahead at the edge of the woods and I quicken my pace slightly. The footsteps accelerated quickly and before I could react I was grabbed from behind. My assailant spun me around and slammed my back into a tree. His arm crossed my throat, cutting off my air. I managed to rip his arm away, but he held me pinned against the tree trunk.

He just held me there for several moments, saying nothing. He looked to be in his mid-forties, but it was difficult to tell in the dim light. He was quite strong.

"What do you want?" I asked, unable to bear his silence any longer. My voice trembled with fear.

"I've been looking for you for a long time, Dorian Gray."

I tensed at the name.

"You have the wrong..."

I doubled over in pain as his fist struck my stomach.

"You killed my brother. It took me a long time to figure it all out. His death made no sense, until my mother passed on and I found Caleb's journal among her things. He killed himself because of you."

"If your brother killed himself then he is responsible for his death, no one else."

I received a slug to the jaw for my comment.

"You thought you could get away with it, didn't you? You pretended to love him and then you turned on him and destroyed him."

I nearly shouted "I did love him!" but that would have given away all. In desperation, I brought my knee up. I meant to knee James Black, for this was surely he, in the groin and make my escape, but I missed. The momentary pain in his leg allowed me to escape, but I didn't get far. In moments I was firmly within his grip once more.

"You took his life and now I'm going to take yours."

James pulled out a knife.

"You're making a mistake!" I said. "You're making a horrible mistake! I'm not this Dorian you seek! When did this happen? When did your brother die?"

"Twenty-eight years ago, what of it?"

The knife loomed closer to my neck.

"Take me into the light! Take me into the light and look at my face! You're about to commit murder! You're about to kill someone who is innocent!"

I pleaded with him, tears streaming from my eyes.

James held the knife close to my throat and pulled me into the light of the nearest street lamp.

"I'm eighteen!" I said crying. "I'm just a freshman! I hadn't even been born yet when your brother died!"

James looked at me in confusion. I could tell he recognized me, could not make sense of my appearance for I had not aged a day. I should have looked like I was in my mid-40s, but my youth was perfectly preserved.

James dropped the knife and stepped back in horror.

"I'm so sorry! I almost... I thought... I was sure...but you can't be. You can't be him!"

His horrified expression told me James truly believed I was not the Dorian who had caused his brother's death. Indeed, I was not. I was the Dorian who had known and loved his brother, but it was his brother who decided to take his own life.

I was still crying and shaking. I'd come so very close to death. I assumed I could be killed. I did not know if the painting could protect me from accident or murder. I did not want to find out.

"I'm sorry!"

"Just let me go. Just let me walk away," I said.

"Yes. Yes, of course! Please forgive me."

I quickly walked away. James was dangerous to me as long as I was near him. At any moment I could say something that would give me away. I'd nearly done it once already. I left Dunn's Woods and walked quickly across campus to the nearest bus stop. There, I caught a ride to McNutt North, my home on campus this time around.

I felt more at ease once I was on the campus bus, surrounded by a few other students. My heart-rate slowed to normal and my breathing calmed down. James Black had taken me by surprise. I never dreamed I'd see him after all these years. I had kept an eye out for him in the years right after Caleb's death. I didn't truly expect him to come after me, but I knew he was suspicious of me when I'd met him. As the months after Caleb's suicide slipped away, so did my concerns about his elder brother. Within a few years I'd forgotten about him entirely, until he stepped out of the shadows with a knife.

I had stopped trembling by the time the bus stopped near McNutt Quad. I thought I'd handled the situation very well. I had almost slipped once, but I'd caught myself in time and I'd had the good sense to get away as quickly as possible so as not to risk another slip. I smiled. James Black would not trouble me again. My ever-youthful face and form had saved me. He truly believed I was not his brother's former lover. Even better, he thought he'd nearly killed an innocent boy. He would likely still seek out the man he believed killed his brother, but he would not find him. He sought an older man who did not exist, except in the painting carefully locked away in my downtown apartment.

Perhaps I should have changed my name. It was too easy to find me. I had spent an enormous amount of money establishing a paper trail for the new Dorian Gray, but perhaps I should have left that name and Bloomington behind. I was attached to this town, however, and even more so to Seth and Daulton. I had foolishly remained friends with them. They both marveled at my youthful appearance. How long before they suspected it was unnatural or did they already?

I had considered these very things before, but I loved Bloomington too much to leave it. It was foolish, I know. I could have lived in New York or Los Angeles or London. I loved big cities. Paris was one of my favorites, but Paris and all the rest were places to visit, not reside.

I walked to McNutt North. This time around my dorm was several blocks north of my old one, Read. It was very near Assembly Hall and the Memorial Stadium. I was wiser this time around in my choice of rooms. I had a private room, but not a suite. My room was the type that any student could obtain if he was willing to pay extra for a single. My suite in Read had raised a lot of questions, even though I didn't allow many others to enter. Of course, the first time I attended IU I had little to hide. I truly was eighteen. I moved into an off-campus apartment my junior year. While I stayed around for eight years completing two degrees, no one was suspicious. I merely looked young for a grad student.

I doubted anyone would connect me to my earlier incarnation. The impossibility of my situation would be enough to cause anyone to dismiss a connection as ludicrous. Only a few professors remained from my earlier years at IU and they were unlikely to remember Dorian Gray.

I walked into my dorm room and turned on the lights. It was small, but I had brought in my own furnishings. There was no separate study this time. There was no kitchen area. There wasn't much of anything, but it would do. I kept an apartment downtown, so I'd spend much of my time there anyway. That is where I kept my fine furniture, my paintings, and my arms collection. I had developed a fondness for antique daggers and swords.

I looked around the little dorm room. I'd brought in nice pieces, but not too nice or out of place. It looked like the room of a college boy who had wealthy parents. I had an IU championship banner on the wall, a football schedule, and an IU calendar. Anyone would came in the room wouldn't suspect I was not just another student.

I kept the portrait secreted away in my downtown apartment, in the study where I kept my arms collection. There was no place to hide it in my dorm room and I did not particularly like to look at it anymore. Sometimes, I felt drawn to it and had to look, but mostly I tried to ignore it. It was locked away and covered with black satin. No one but me had laid eyes on it since the day it was delivered to Read all those years ago.

The last time I'd looked at Dorian in the portrait his hair was thinning and creases were beginning to be evident on his face. He was not yet old, but he looked the age I was supposed to be. What disturbed me most was the cruel look at the corners of the eyes, the accusing glare, and the sneer. I felt as if he was staring at me, condemning me for forcing him to bear not only my age, but my sins. No matter what angle I looked at him, he stared straight at me. Perhaps it was my imagination. Perhaps not. I could let no other view the portrait so I could seek out no opinions on the matter.

Sometimes, at night especially, I felt the painting calling to me. There was no voice or sound, but I could feel it summoning me to look upon it. Mostly, I tried to ignore it, but then tossed and turned and had bad dreams. Sometimes, I unlocked the door, uncovered the portrait, and gazed at it. It was at those times that the portrait nearly screamed "See what you have done to me?"

I had to look for a few moments only, then I could cover my sins once more, go to sleep, and rest well. The portrait was satisfied, until the next time.

I hoped the portrait would not trouble me in my dorm room. It was only a few blocks away, but perhaps it would let me rest here.

I had spent many years away from campus life and this time I intended to focus more on the social aspect. I had been far too studious during my first round of college. I did not intend to shirk on attending classes or studying, but I had no great desire to immerse myself as I did the first time. I now possessed the advantage of many years of wisdom. I already knew much and could therefore study less. In addition, for the first couple of years most of my courses would be ones I had taken before. My freshman and sophomore years would be mostly review.

With my new agenda in mind. I walked out of McNutt, up to 17th Street and headed west, cutting across the parking lots by Assembly Hall and the Memorial Stadium. Varsity Villas just west of the stadium was my destination. I was certain I could find a party there as well as a young college boy to seduce.

Chapter Fifteen:
Dorian Enslaves a Straight Boy

October 2010

I sat at my laptop and typed another name into my list, "Mike 19, straight." Since the beginning of the semester I'd kept a list, by date, of the boys I'd seduced or who I had allowed to seduce me. It was a rare date when there wasn't at least one name listed and quite often there were two or even three. I'd been involved in a few three-ways, but none so memorable as those Gabrial and I once arranged. I could have had many, many more but I was selective. The dates that had no names under them were blank entirely by choice.

Hooking up had become even easier than it had been in the early 1980s. There were hookup sites like Manhunt and Adam4Adam and smart-phone apps like Grindr. I had no trouble attracting boys at parties and on campus, but I found it fun to use new technology to obtain a boy. It was like a catalog of hunks. Just place an order and minutes later he appears at the door.

My biggest problem online was the huge volume of unwanted emails and messages. The old and unattractive pursued me, many offering me money to have sex with them. Sometimes, the offers were rather substantial. I knew of a few boys who earned extra money by doing some escorting of that sort, but I had no need of cash. I had more than ever before and I had long had more than I could possibly spend. It piled up and up in my bank accounts no matter how much I might spend.

I did not show my face on the internet hookup sites. I did not want to be bothered by strangers in public any more than I already was every day. I posted a full-length, shirtless shot instead. I had kept up working out as a hobby after Gabrial had shown me the ropes all those years ago. I was careful not to bulk up, but had maintained just the right amount of toned muscle. I could never be mistaken for a jock, but I was firm, and smooth, and trim. My body was defined and oozed sensuality. I often nearly laughed when guys met me and viewed my face for the first time. Their expression told me they almost couldn't believe that someone with such a fine-looking body could also possess a face of such extraordinary beauty.

I grinned. Mike was straight. I knew it without a doubt and yet I'd seduced him. He was nineteen but no guy had ever gone down on him before. Not only did I seduce him into letting me blow him, but he'd wrapped his lips around my cock. Straight guys didn't give good head, but the very idea of a straight boy serving me on his knees more than compensated for his lack of expertise. The greatest pleasure would come the next time my path crossed Mike's. He'd have to look me in the eye knowing he'd given me head. IU was a large university, but I always made sure I knew enough about the straight boys I seduced so that a post-sex encounter would occur. Then, I could enjoy the look of guilt, shame, and remorse that crossed the features of my latest conquest. That look was as satisfying as the sex itself.

Some guys claimed to be straight, but weren't. I could always could always pick out the pretenders and separate them from the true straight boys. That was the advantage of experience. While I enjoyed hooking up with any attractive guy, I particularly liked getting my hands on a straight boy. I also enjoyed "total tops" who I could bend over and fuck. I liked getting into the pants of boys with boyfriends or girlfriends, too. I enjoyed the challenge and the forbidden. A dozen or more gay boys a day would drop to their knees for me, but the straight boys and those in relationships were more of a challenge. I was a predator. I lived for the hunt.

There seemed to be a good deal more gay boys at IU than there had been a quarter of a century before. Then again, perhaps it was merely that more of them were out. Gays were accepted at IU in the 1980s, but now...they were so accepted that being gay wasn't a big deal. During my previous college years being gay and out gave one a certain notoriety, but no more. There was no novelty in it. A large number of students identified as bi. The world was changing.

My classes were a breeze. I was amazed at how much came back to me from my previous college years. The information was still in my brain, even though I hadn't realized it. It was as if my mind was a computer with hidden files that revealed themselves when needed. I found my years of life-experience just as valuable, perhaps more so. There truly was wisdom in years and I was uniquely suited to understand that. No other eighteen-year-old on campus had over forty years of experience to draw upon. Not only the knowledge, but the discipline to sit down and get reading and other assignments done was valuable. I'd never been a procrastinator, but now I fully understood the value of getting work finished and out of the way.

I truly possessed the best of both worlds, plus eternal youth, a beautiful body and face, and virtually endless wealth. No one deserved to have it all I supposed, but since I did possess it all I wasn't going to argue or even ponder the point. As Seth had taught me long ago, life was for living and enjoying, not analyzing.

My lack of difficulties with my schoolwork left me the time I desired for socializing. While seduction was nearly an obsession with me, I also liked to party. With my looks and charm I could attend any party on or off campus, invited or not. Gay boys and older gays flocked to me. Straight boys liked to use me as bait. Girls were drawn to me and being near me gave poor, pathetic straight boys a chance to meet and hit on them. I was publicly out, but there were girls who didn't know about me yet and there were others who were still interested in hanging out with me, even though they knew I'd never fuck them. There were yet more girls who believed that they could seduce me even though I was gay. I was surrounded by girls. Straight boys had learned that if they wanted to score, a good place to do so was near Dorian Gray.

I didn't mind being used, for that is how a few of those straight boys fell into my snare. If they gazed upon my beauty too long some began to wonder what it would be like with me and then I had them.

There were other opportunities with the straight boys too. Their raging hormones and lust for women drove them to do things they would otherwise not contemplate. I knew such a situation was upon me at yet another late night party when I laid eyes on Evan, a horny freshman I'd noticed in my English Composition 101 class. He was devouring Shara, an especially attractive blond girl who had long lusted after me, with his eyes.

Evan was blond, buff, and quite obviously a horny jock. No doubt he'd worked his way through the females at his high school and was continuing to work his magic in college. I sensed he was like me, only the prey he pursued was female.

I watched with great amusement as he tried to charm the girl who made his groin ache with lust and longing. It was a bit like watching a nature program as the boy strutted his stuff. He was dressed for the hunt in a too-tight shirt that revealed his broad shoulders and muscular pecs. His biceps strained his sleeves and his cock strained the front of his jeans. I had observed him long enough to know he was straight.

I selected the strutting stud as my prey. Straight and gorgeous—it was a combination I couldn't resist. An evil grin curled the corners of my mouth. If this young, blond, stud-muffin had any idea of what I had planned for him he would have run away screaming.

I looked at the girl until she noticed my attention. I gave her a smile and she broke away from her pursuer. He frowned, but took a drink from his cup and pretended not to be annoyed. I whispered in the girl's ear and we both gazed at the young jock. He looked back at us with a question in his eyes. The girl and I shared a whispered conversation and then I left her, walked to my latest car, a metallic blue Lotus Exige Cup 260, and waited.

The pair were not long in coming. I knew Shara could lead Evan around by the dick and I'd promised her something I knew she both wanted desperately and never thought she'd get. Shara had tried for me before, but I'd always politely rebuffed her, until now. We had cut a deal that would give us both what we wanted, Evan too, although he would pay a price. If he had any idea of how high that price would become he would not have been grinning lustfully at Shara.

"Holy fuck! What a car!" Evan said.

I grinned. My Lotus had landed me more than one boy. The straight boys in particular could not resist a $100,000 sports car.

"Get in," I said. "I'm afraid you'll both have to squeeze into one seat, but we won't be going far."

I knew Evan wouldn't mind having Shara pressed hard against his lap.

"You're in my English Comp class, right?" Evan asked as I started up the sports car.

"Yes, I'm Dorian Gray."

"Evan Belmont. Fuck! I can't get over this car!"

I merely smiled at the ability of my Lotus to take Evan's mind off Shara. Perhaps I could have bagged Evan with the Lotus alone, but no, I'd analyzed him and knew getting in his pants would take extreme measures.

I took the pair not to my tiny dorm room in McNutt, but downtown to my apartment in The Kirkwood. Both were suitably impressed.

"It's my parents," I explained. "They use it rarely. I come here to get away from campus and for...other activities."

I made them both a drink, although they were each already a little tipsy. I flipped a hidden switch and my spy cams began recording. I often liked to relive certain sexual encounters and this time I had more devilish plans.

I let Shara and Evan into my bedroom. I knew Evan would be extremely nervous so I turned to Shara and kissed her. Tonight would be a new experience for me as well as for Evan. I was going to have sex with a girl. The idea had never appealed to me and yet it was the ultimate perversion for me.

Shara and I made out. I let her pull my shirt over my head. She began to caress, then lick my chest. It was too much for Evan. He pulled off his shirt, revealing his ripped torso, and walked toward us. Shara began to feel his pecs and washboard abs even as she sucked on my nipples. After a bit, she turned her lips to Evan's chest. He gazed at me over her blond hair as she sucked his nipples. His eyes were glazed over with lust. I had learned long ago that lust was the ultimate drug. I never bothered with minor drugs because I had access to the most powerful of all.

Shara stood and made out first with me, then Evan. Kissing a girl was an odd sensation and yet not all that different from making out with a boy. I didn't feel the intense lust I felt with a boy and yet it was pleasurable.

I moved to kiss Evan and he pulled back. Shara pouted and Evan crumbled. I pressed my lips to his and kissed him. I grasped the back of his head and held him in place while I forced my tongue into his mouth.

"That's so hot," Shara said. "You boys are making me so wet."

That encouraged Evan to kiss me more deeply. I nearly laughed. Girls could make straight boys do anything. When Shara pulled Evan's mouth to hers I gave her a grin. She was holding up her end of the bargain well.

Shara took the lead and slowly stripped herself and then both of us. Soon, we were all completely naked. I was not attracted to Shara and Evan was not attracted to me, but both Evan and myself were hard and throbbing. There was something each of us wanted here. Shara got the best deal because she alone was making no compromise. I had little doubt she would have slept with Evan sooner or later and I knew she wanted me. I intended to come out of the situation with the very most, but neither of my partners knew anything about that. Shara would never know. After tonight, I would be done with her unless I someday needed her to ensnare another reluctant straight boy.

Shara demonstrated her head-giving skills first on me, then Evan. She pulled us close together and moved back and forth between us. Evan's muscular thigh pressed against my own. I put my arm around his shoulder. He tensed, but couldn't pull away without pulling his cock from Shara's mouth.

Shara gave decent head, for a girl. I'd rate her skills above that of straight boys, but well below those of the bi and gay boys. I guess it was true that owning the equipment made one more proficient at operating it. Shara had Evan moaning and groaning loudly. The masculine sounds he uttered turned me on like never before.

The moment of truth came soon. Shara stood, handed me a condom from the box by the bed, and lie back on the bed. I put on the condom and climbed on top of Shara before I could lose my erection. Shara guided me into her. I closed my eyes and pretended she was Evan. She wasn't nearly tight enough to be his jock-boy ass, but I maintained the fantasy and began to thrust.

I could hear Evan breathing hard. He was no doubt chomping at the bit for his turn and getting wildly turned on by watching me fuck the girl he so desired. It didn't matter that I was gay at that point. Evan was watching a male-female couple go at it. I did my best to give Shara a good fuck. This was her payment and I always paid well. Shara would walk away tonight with the knowledge that she was the only girl I'd ever fucked and likely the only girl I ever would. She had what thousands of other girls had desired over the years.

I kept thrusting and picturing Evan beneath me. Shara's moans made it difficult, but I pretended someone else was doing her right next to me. I lost myself in the fantasy, thrust harder and harder, and then I exploded deep inside her with a loud groan.

"Who says gay boys can't fuck?" Shara said, smiling.

Shara stood. Evan made a move for a condom, but Shara grasped his wrist.

"I want to watch the two of you first."

Evan's face paled.

"Oral only."

"I don't..."

Shara placed her finger on Evan's lips, then ran it down over his hard torso. She whispered in his ear and he swallowed hard. Whatever she said to him made his cock throb.

I moved in, sank to my knees, and pulled Evan's cock into the first male mouth it had ever entered. I showed him the skills of a true gay boy. He couldn't help but moan as I gave him what was probably the best head he'd ever experienced.

When I had him worked up to the point of popping his load I pulled off. I needed him out-of-control horny for what came next.

I stood. Shara placed a hand on his shoulder and pushed down. He resisted, but then gazed into her eyes and began to sink to his knees. In moments, Evan pulled my cock into his mouth, tasting his first dick ever.

He did not know it, but I had him now. No matter what happened after, he was mine.

Evan was one lousy cocksucker. I wasn't sure if he was just that bad or if he was doing a horrible job on purpose. If he thought I was going to ask him to stop he was out of his mind. The very fact that he was there, on his knees, slobbering on my dick was enough to make it hot. Evan looked incredibly sexy giving me head. I began to moan louder and despite Evan's lack of oral expertise my orgasm shot through my body. Evan took the first shot in the mouth. He pulled off quickly and spit, but the next shots got him in the face. He looked mad enough to chew on nails and I nearly laughed in his face. He jumped to his feet, fists clenched, muscles bulging.

Shara grabbed him and shoved her tongue in his mouth. They kissed their way back onto the bed, where Evan fell upon Shara. I handed him a condom. It was time for the straight boy to get his reward. He'd be paying for it dearly enough.

I stood back and watched as the straight couple got it in. Evan was as good at fucking as he was bad at sucking. He made Shara moan and squeal with delight. I'd never been into straight porn, but the pair of them excited me as they got it on. I watched until Evan thrust deep, moaned, and his face contorted with pure pleasure. Shara shouted out his name. She might have been faking, but if so it was a fine job of acting.

We dressed. I asked Shara and Evan if they'd like a ride back to campus, but Evan offered to walk Shara and she accepted. I let them out, then showered.

Before returning to McNutt, I unlocked my study and uncovered the portrait. Dorian looked just as wicked as ever, but this time he looked more lecherous than anything. It was an ugly expression on his forty-something face. We sneered at each other and I covered him once more.

**

The expression on Evan's face in the next class we shared was in itself worth hooking up with a girl. If I had to describe it with one word that word would be mortified. Evan couldn't look me in the eyes. When he did, I read a mixture of anger, guilt, shame, and humiliation there. Added to this was a touch of arousal, no doubt created by his memories of banging Shara.

I didn't drop the bomb on him immediately. I gave him a few days to suffer with remorse. I wanted the unpleasant memories to fade a bit before I opened the wounds wide. Besides, it took a little time to prepare the demonstration what would make it obvious to even a straight jock that he belonged to me now. I had learned much about computers and websites over the years, but I tended to hire others to do technological things for me. This project I wanted and needed to handle all by myself.

I kept myself busy with boys, schoolwork, eating out, working out, and just generally enjoying life as much as humanly possible. It was two full weeks before I stopped Evan as he entered our shared classroom and told him I wanted to talk to him after class. He started to protest, but then clamped his mouth shut when he saw the expression on my face.

I couldn't help but smile all through class at how I was about to change Evan's life. He would no doubt think I was destroying it, but no, I only want to play with him for a while, not forever. By the end of the school year at the latest I'd tire of him and go onto another toy.

"So? What is it?" Evan impatiently after class. "I have to get to the SRSC to work out."

"Only this," I said, handing him a slip of paper with my phone number, a website address, and a password.

"What's this?"

"Check it out when you get to a computer, but view it privately or you'll be sorry. You'll need the password. No one can access the site without it...for now."

Evan eyed me, more confused than anything.

"I expect to hear from you tonight."

Evan nervously shifted from one foot to the other. I enjoyed his discomfort. I was going to enjoy what was coming even more.

I went about my day thinking now and then of Evan. Had he used the password and checked out the website yet? I would have given a good deal just to watch his face when his eyes fell on the screen.

My cell didn't ring until 9 p.m. It was Evan.

"What do you want?" he immediately asked.

"I want you to come to my dorm room now and we'll discuss the details here."

I told him I was in McNutt and told him to meet me at the main entrance. He arrived in less than ten minutes, looking frightened and angry. We did not speak until we were in my dorm room.

"So you hide cameras in your parent's apartment? You sick faggot. If you so much as...."

"Shut up, Evan. You're in no position to make threats. You're going to do what I tell you or I'll remove the password from the website and post the address on Facebook. What will all your buddies think when they see pictures and video of you sucking cock?"

"You know why I did it!"

"Yes, I do, because you were thinking with your dick. You wanted Shara so bad you'd do anything to get her. You got her, but it's going to cost you more than you thought."

"Is Shara in on this? I can't believe..."

"No. Shara wanted me and I wanted you. My price for having sex with her was you. She doesn't know anything about the cams. She had no idea I had plans for you beyond some mutual oral."

"So what do you want, money? Is that how you pay for that fancy car? You set up straight boys and then blackmail them?"

"I don't need your money. I have more money than I can spend in a lifetime. That apartment isn't my parents. It belongs to me."

"If you don't want money then...."

Evan jerked his head in my direction and stared.

"No," he said.

"Yes," I said grinning evilly. "From now on, you're my bitch."

"Please, man. Please, don't."

"You're too hard to resist, Evan. You're gorgeous and you're straight. I've had a lot of hot guys, but very few straight boys. Guys like you are rare and therefore valuable."

"If I refuse?"

"You know what happens. In less than twenty-four hours everyone will know you're a closet fag."

"But I'm not!"

"Then why were you sucking my cock?"

"You fucking know why!"

"Yeah, you're right. I do. No one else knows. You can tell them, of course. Shara might even back you up, but it won't matter. Everyone will know you're a cocksucker and most will just assume the 'I did it to get a girl' excuse is a lie."

"I fucking hate you!"

"Hate me all you want. It only makes it better."

Evan smacked his fist into his palm and growled in frustration.

"If I do what you want..."

"No one will ever see the website."

"How do I know you'll keep your word?"

"You don't, but you don't have any choice."

"How long do I have to do as you say?"

"Until I get tired of you, this school year at the most, maybe less."

"Until next May?"

"At the longest, although you are extremely hot, Evan, so I may want you that long."

Evan clinched his jaw and looked out the window, then looked back at me.

"I don't have a choice, do I?"

"You have a choice. You don't have to do anything I say if you don't mind that website going public. Gays are quite accepted and I'm sure you can take care of yourself. Of course, everyone on campus will see the pics and vid of you sucking dick. Perhaps the video will go viral. Maybe your friends back home will even take a look."

"Okay! Damn you! Okay!"

I smiled.

"Take off your shirt."

"Now? Can't we..."

"Now, Evan."

Evan pulled off his shirt, revealing his broad, muscled shoulders, hard pecs, and defined abs. He was a gorgeous eighteen-year-old straight boy and he was all mine. He was my personal sex toy. I should have thought of blackmail long ago. Straight boys and their irrational fears made it so easy.

I directed Evan in a striptease. As every item of clothing came off, revealing more and more of his hard, sculpted body, my lust for him increased. When he was down to his boxer-briefs, I walked over to him, pulled him to me and forced my tongue into his mouth. Evan resisted at first, but a glare let him know that struggling against the inevitable would only prolong his torment.

I stripped off my shirt, pulled Evan to me, and kissed him again. Evan was a great kisser. His lips and tongue never ceased moving. I hugged him close, feeling the hard muscles of his pecs pressing into me. Something else was pressing into me as well.

"I think you're getting into doing it with a guy. *This* tells me you are," I said, groping the growing bulge in his boxer-briefs.

I knew that Evan's arousal was a natural reaction to body contact and making out, but I enjoyed a good mind-fuck. Any little bit of pleasure Even derived from contact with me would put doubts in his mind. I was absolutely certain Evan was straight, but now he wasn't so sure. I was going to enjoy messing with his mind almost as much as I'd enjoy his hard, sexy body.

I traveled down Evan's torso, admiring it with my hands, lips, and tongue. I indulged my every whim. I'd seduce straight boys, but they were often inebriated and the encounters brief. Now, I had a captive straight boy and I could take my time.

I stripped Evan naked, got on my knees, and gave him head. I used my twenty-plus years of experience to give him the best blow he'd ever had. Moans and whimpers of pleasure escaped from his lips despite himself. He began to thrust into my mouth. I gripped Evan's firm butt-cheeks. Damn! They were as firm as his pecs! I used all my talents to make Evan feel better than he'd ever felt before. He began to moan more loudly and then he exploded into my mouth.

When I stood, a blush colored Evan's cheeks.

"You definitely liked that," I said, then grinned wickedly.

I made Evan flex his muscles for me. I ran my hands over his biceps and pecs as he did so. His body was magnificent. I couldn't resist leaning over and sucking on his nipples. A whimper escaped his lips again. Evan would definitely be questioning his sexuality now. I grinned just thinking of the mental torment.

I got so worked up fondling and groping Evan that I was hard and throbbing. I stood back and admired Evan's incredible physique.

"Get on your knees."

Evan reluctantly replied. I walked toward him.

"Suck it."

Evan balked. He shook his head.

"Your choice," I said, walking to my laptop.

"What...what are you doing?"

"I'm removing the password from your website then I'm going to email the link to a few friends. Within an hour..."

"No, please!"

I just stared at Evan, then down at my cock.

"Please," he begged. Tears began to roll down his cheeks.

"Choose," I said. "You have five seconds. I'm not going to waste my time waiting on you."

Evan crossed the short distance between us, still on his knees. He leaned in, opened his mouth, and pulled me in. Tears still ran down his cheeks, further evidence he was definitely a straight boy.

Evan had given a lousy blow when he sucked me so he could have Shara. This time, I gave him direction and smacked his face hard if I felt teeth.

"You're going to suck it until you make me cum so do it right!" I ordered.

I could tell he was trying. He was getting a little better. With time, he'd learn.

Like before, I got off on looking down and seeing a straight boy on his knees serving me. This time, the head was better. I'd wondered during the three-way if Evan was purposely giving me bad head, but no, I was now sure he was merely inexperienced and unenthusiastic. He was improving.

I grabbed Evan's head and thrust into his mouth, stopping just short of making him gag. I got off on the domination. Evan was my slave boy to do with as I pleased. Of course, I couldn't be too horrible to him. What I forced him to do had to be a lesser evil in his eyes than having the entire campus watch him suck cock online. I had to be careful not to go too far. Of course, I had no plans for anything so severe he'd rather be exposed than endure the torment. My plans for Evan were all sexual. Only his mind would be tortured—with doubts about his sexuality and that torment would be entirely his own doing. I'd merely plant the seeds of doubt. Evan would nurture them.

"If you don't get me off by giving me head my dick is going into your virgin ass," I said.

That scared him. I did indeed plan to fuck Evan, but not tonight. There were some things I wanted to save for later. I wanted to move slowly and enjoy every moment of using my straight boy toy.

Evan's lips and tongue were getting me increasingly excited. My threat had done the trick. He was now properly motivated to do his best. Evan's best was sub-par. Any gay boy, even a virgin, could have done better. Still, the mere fact he was straight made it...

I moaned loudly. I grabbed Evan's head and forced him down on my cock as I exploded into his mouth. My orgasm spread throughout my body. I held Evan in place even after I'd finished shooting. I forced him to swallow.

I pushed Evan away.

"You can go now. I'll tell you when I want you again."

"You won't...tell anyone about this, will you?"

"Of course not. Your intense need to keep what you've done with me a secret is what makes it possible for me to control you. If I told anyone about what I forced you to do I'd lose my power over you. You can't seriously be stupid enough to think I'd expose you unless you defied me."

Evans cheeks flushed with anger. He was strong enough to break me in half, but he was impotent against me. He was my bitch.

"Now get out. I'm done with you for now."

Evan did as he was told without another word. I grinned as he closed the door. I was going to thoroughly enjoy my new toy. I'd tire of him, of course, and Evan could be thankful for that. I did intend to keep my word. When I was done using him, I would remove the website and keep the video solely for my own viewing pleasure. Of course, if he defied me, it would be rather interesting to see what happened when everyone started watching him have sex with another guy online. Who ever said straight boys weren't fun?

***

Looking Evan in the eye during the next class we shared was even more fun than doing so after the three-way. Evan knew I held his life in my hands. I could out him on a whim. It didn't matter that he was straight, few would believe it once they viewed the photos and video of Evan giving head. It was Evan's stupidity as much as his insecurity that allowed me to control him. Gays were quite accepted at IU and in Bloomington in general. If exposed, Evan wouldn't face any beatings. It was doubtful he'd even be called names. It would be difficult to face his friends, and some of his jock buddies might give him a hard time, but I had the feeling even they would tend to be understanding. There would also be legal repercussions for me, but I doubted Evan had even considered that. I loved them young, hung, and stupid. It truly was Evan's own stupidity and fears that made him my slave. If he had any sense at all he would have looked me in the eyes and said, "Do your worst."

I didn't know if I would have exposed Evan or not had he defied me. I might have done so just to see what happened, although the ensuing drama might have been anti-climactic. If he'd stood up to me and shown me he had balls I might have respected him enough to simply make the website go away. I could be generous at times. Then again, it would have been fun to watch him suffer.

Evan had not defied me and now I owned him. I enjoyed that. I made a mental note to purchase a collar and leash. Evan would look good on a leash. I wanted most of our sessions to be at my apartment too. I wanted my time with Evan on video, not for further blackmail, but for my own private enjoyment.

Evan was nervous and fearful around me. He actually flinched if I drew close, fearful I would demand he serve me again. I let him be for several days. While I got off on using him, I didn't want to tire of him quickly. Evan was a toy I planned to play with only occasionally. Boys were easy to seduce, at least for me. I seldom had to work at it. Usually, it was merely a matter of saying 'yes' when propositioned. I could have taken a college boy back to my dorm room every night if I wished, but I did have other interests.

Chapter Sixteen: Dorian Uses His Boy Toy

November 2010

I spent a good deal of time in Daulton's studio. It was still in the same place after all these years. I did not allow him to paint me, for I did not know if a second portrait would affect the first. What if any portrait Daulton painted of me would reveal my age and sins? I could not risk such a portrait being viewed by anyone but myself. It was best not to take chances. Daulton complained, of course, and tried his best to convince me to sit for him, but on that point I would not budge.

"You really should let me see the portrait I did of you all those years ago," Daulton said just after I'd turned down yet another request to paint my likeness.

"I'm not comfortable letting anyone see it, Daulton. Surely, you can understand. You once said you put so much of yourself in it that you didn't think you'd ever exhibit it. There is far too much of me in it as well. I cannot bear for anyone else to view it, not even you."

Daulton sighed.

"Besides, why do you need to look at a portrait of me when I'm sitting right here in your studio?"

"I detest when your logic makes sense, Dorian."

"My logic always makes sense."

"You sound far too much like Seth!"

"I consider that a compliment."

Daulton grunted.

"You thought he was a bad influence on me. I think I've turned out rather well."

"He was and is a bad influence on you and everyone else. I love him dearly, but he's a destroyer of lives."

"Nonsense. Look at me. Do I look destroyed?"

"You look...unchanged Dorian. It's as if you haven't aged a day since I painted your likeness. What's your secret?"

I stiffened for a moment, but quickly recovered.

"I never smoke."

"Neither do I and I get older by the moment."

"Oh, you look just fine, Daulton."

"Liar."

I grinned.

"Oh, I want to commission you. Would you be up for painting some of the landmarks of Bloomington? I'd like some paintings of the Sample Gates, the Rose Well House, and such, whatever catches your eye. I want paintings that are distinctly Bloomington."

"Of course, I can come up with some wonderful subjects. I painted a view of the Rose Well House before."

"You did? Why did I never get to see it?"

"Because it was snatched up before I even finished it. One of the professors walked by and struck a deal with me. The moment it was finished, I delivered it to him."

"Well, no selling to anyone but me this time."

"You have my word, Dorian. You've been most generous in supporting my art."

"You have been most generous in allowing me to purchase your amazing creations with mere money."

Daulton smiled. I enjoyed the easy banter between us. I could rest easy with Daulton. I never worried about impressing anyone, but with him my guard was completely down. Well, it was down as much as possible and more than with anyone else.

I remained with Daulton for some hours as he painted. He was working on a view of his own garden through the French doors. Daulton often painted scenes from his own garden and it always amazed me that he could draw so many different subjects from the same place. He'd once told me he could paint only his garden for the rest of his life and never create two paintings that looked alike. I believed him. He was truly a talented artist.

When I left the studio, I walked back to The Kirkwood. It was only a short walk and I'd left my Lotus parked the garage under the luxury apartment building.

Daulton was truly a good soul. He was completely dedicated to his art. I often wondered if it was that dedication that made his portrait of me alive. I owed Daulton a great deal. If it wasn't for him I'd now be a middle-age man with wrinkles and thinning hair. I regretted that I could never tell him the truth of the matter. I showed my appreciation in other ways. I made sure he never wanted for cash. If I even suspected he was low on funds I went to his studio and purchased some of his work. I always paid handsomely and yet what I purchased was well worth the cost. I couldn't possibly display all the paintings in my apartment, so I gave them as gifts and donated them to charity auctions. I might be wicked, but I was far from all bad.

I walked into my apartment. I was surrounded by Daulton's art, fine furnishes, and all my favorite pieces. My apartment was such a contrast to my dorm room in McNutt. Still, I enjoyed the double life. I enjoyed playing a college boy. Most were only able to experience their college years once. I could do so over and over.

My smile faded. I could hear him calling to me, not in words, but I could hear him nonetheless. I resisted, but then gave in. If I didn't, he would keep at me and at me until I submitted. If I went to sleep before doing so, he would enter my dreams.

I unlocked the study and walked inside, passing the antique swords, sabers, and daggers on display. I pulled away the black satin cover and recoiled, even though I knew what to expect. Each time I gazed on Dorian his ugliness struck me like a blow to the chest. Was this really me? Was this truly what I was? He looked older than his forty-odd years. The once youthful and beautiful features had been warped and perverted into an ugly caricature of me.

Surely I wasn't that bad? I hadn't killed anyone. Yes, Caleb had killed himself over me, but he made the choice to die. I didn't force him into that noose at gunpoint. I hadn't raped anyone. Yeah, I'd fucked a few guys without permission, but if they really cared they wouldn't have allowed themselves to get so inebriated that it could happen. I'd merely taken advantage of circumstance the way so many straight guys had taken advantage of girls. It was justice of a sort. There was a big difference from what I'd done and raping some twelve-year-old boy, which I had not done and would never do. I had hooked up with a few high school boys, but none younger and it had always been consensual...mostly. Blackmailing Evan into sex wasn't an act of kindness, but it was his kind who tormented gay boys the world over. Using him was payback in the name of all the gay boys who had been pushed around, bullied, and called names. I had sexually used a lot of guys, but they knew they were being used. I made no commitments or promises. If I never called or texted them again I hadn't cheated them. Most guys would give just about anything to get with me once. By letting them blow me or bend over for me I was doing them a favor.

I didn't pretend to be a nice guy, but I wasn't evil. The Dorian who gazed at me from the portrait did indeed look evil. He looked as if he'd like to step out of the painting, wrap his fingers around my neck, and squeeze until he'd squeezed the life out of me. He looked as he if had murdered and raped. I shook my head. No. This could not be the real me.

I walked across the room and gazed into the mirror as I often did after viewing the picture. I was young and beautiful. I was forever eighteen. No wicked deeds were etched upon my features. If anything, I looked angelic. I looked back at the portrait. Dorian's eyes stared at me accusingly. They called me a liar. They said 'look at me for I am you.' I turned away. I would not believe it.

***

I didn't call on Evan to be my play-thing until two weeks had passed. Perhaps he thought I'd never use him again, but even he was too smart for that. He came to my dorm room obediently, but I took him from there to my apartment. I made him strip off his shirt and fitted him with a spiked collar and a leash. He looked so fucking hot in the part of a slave boy that I had to stop and lick all over his chest.

I stripped him and used his body for my pleasure. I took my time and explored him from head to toe. I took off my clothes and used his mouth. I tied his hands firmly behind his back and commented that I could kill him and there was no way he could stop me. I had no intention of killing him, but the momentary fear in his eyes was satisfying. I truly could take his life if I wanted. His hard muscles were useless with his wrists tied behind his back. I wondered what it would be like to kill someone, but I wondered only.

I explored Evan's magnificent body to my heart's content. The bondage turned me on. He was under my control with or without bonds and yet the rope binding his wrists added an extra erotic element to our sex-play.

I hauled Evan to his feet by the hair and threw him down on my bed. I climbed on top of him and rubbed my hardness between his butt-cheeks.

"What are you doing?"

"You know what I'm doing. You can feel it, can't you?"

"What are you *going* to do then?"

"What do you think I'm going to do?"

"Stop playing games and just answer me!"

I tugged hard on his leash, choking him for a moment.

"Don't raise your voice to me. I own you."

I leaned in until my body was spread out full-length over his and whispered in his ear.

"I'm going to fuck you like you've fucked so many girls in the past."

Evan struggled against the ropes and tried to get up. I shoved him back down.

"I'm going to fuck you, Evan, and there's nothing you can do about it. Even if you did free yourself, I still own you—all of you. You are mine to do with as I please."

"Please don't! Not that! All the rest has been bad enough, but not that!"

"There's no way out, Evan. I'm going to use your hot, hot ass. The only decision you have to make is do you want it with lube or without?"

"Neither."

"If you don't choose, I'll fuck you without and believe me it will hurt more, a lot more."

"Please don't!"

"Chose."

Evan remained silent, except for some very unmanly whimpering.

"Very well, then."

I began to push myself against him.

"With! With!"

I laughed, but got up and generously applied lube. I put the lube away and once more positioned myself for entry.

"The more you fight it, the more it will hurt," I said.

With that I pushed myself inside him. He screamed even though I didn't jam it in as I desired. I merely pushed myself into him slowly, penetrating his virgin ass.

Evan groaned and cried out. He breathed hard and fast. I sank myself into him deeper and deeper until I was all the way in. I savored the moment. I'd impaled a straight boy on my pole. I'd popped his cherry. No one had ever fucked him before and no one but me ever would again.

"You're my bitch now," I moaned into his ear.

I wasn't unnecessarily rough, but I used Evan. I fucked him good and hard. He cried out and sobbed and I knew it was as much from the humiliation of getting fucked than from the pain. Perhaps it was mostly from the humiliation. Surely the pain had subsided already. I knew from experience that bottoming hurt at first and then began to feel good. That would fuck with Evan's mind more than anything...when being used by me began to feel pleasurable.

I had something truly evil planned for Evan—a serious mind fuck. I turned him onto his back, pulled his legs over my shoulders, and penetrated him again. I stared into his eyes as I used him. When he tried to look away I demanded he looked at me. He obeyed. I had another purpose in using this position besides humiliating Evan. I enjoyed watching his beautiful muscles flex as I thrust into him. From this angle I could hit places inside him that Evan didn't even know existed.

Evan began to moan. I smiled. It was starting. Despite his hatred for what I was doing to him his body was reacting. He was beginning to experience the arousal and joy that came with bottoming. Unknown to Evan, I was not only working to create pleasure for myself, but for him as well. His moans became louder and more frequent. I could feel myself getting close, aroused nearly to the breaking point by Evan's own arousal.

Evan moaned louder than ever before. The moment I'd been waiting for came. Without either of us touching his cock even once he fired a massive load all over his own torso and mine. I watched as his eyes rolled up in ecstasy.

"I knew you'd get off on this. In your heart you know you're a fag," I whispered to him.

I went over the edge. I moaned and came inside him, claiming him as my own.

When I was finished, I untied Evan. He quickly pulled on his clothes. His expression was one of confusion, humiliation, and shame. I grinned wickedly. I'd fucked his body and his mind. His thoughts were racing now. He'd try desperately to reconcile his sexual orientation with his orgasm. He could never deny to himself or me that I'd made him cum just by fucking him. Our coupling had lasted only a few minutes, but the mind fuck would go on and on and on.

I experienced a momentary pang of guilt as I closed the door behind Evan. Using him sexually was one thing, playing with his mind was another. He was young and far more naïve than he realized. I'd intentionally planted the seeds of doubt within him. I was quite certain of his sexuality. I knew something Evan did not. Everyone was, in fact, bisexual. Labels like heterosexual and homosexual indicated the two extremes of a scale; those who were far more attracted to one sex than the other. In Evan's mind any attraction to another male, any pleasure that came from sex with another guy, was evidence that his heterosexuality and his very masculinity was in question.

Was it fair to take advantage of his naïveté? Was it right to inflict emotional torment for my own entertainment? Probably not, but then again Evan was nothing more than a toy I used to amuse myself. His magnificent body and his innocent mind were mine to do with as I pleased. If I wasn't meant to use him, he wouldn't have fallen into my hands. For some reason he'd been selected by fate to be used and controlled by me. Perhaps when I was finished with him he would be the better for it. No matter. He amused me and aroused me and I'd play with him until I tired of him. Then, I'd put my toy back on the shelf and he could go on his way.

I showered, washing away the sticky evidence of Evan's orgasm. Seth had been right all those years ago. The world was mine as long as I was young and beautiful. At the time he said it, both Seth and I believed my youth and beauty were fleeting, but we were both wrong there.

Without Seth my life would have been so very different. In my own innocence I hadn't considered the impermanence of either my youth or beauty. Like all, or at least most, of the young, I thought of myself as going on and on never changing. How odd that even surrounded by evidence of aging in others and knowing we would each one day grow old we still failed to comprehend the obvious; that all too soon our youth would be gone. In my case, my original innocent view held true. I would not age. My beauty would not fade. I would go on forever as I was now. I, alone, would continue with the immortal beauty all youths wrongly believed they possessed.

I returned to my dorm after showering. I was tempted to linger in the luxury of my apartment, but I wanted to immerse myself in my role as a college student. I had never lost my love for theater. I had not become an actor upon the stage. That was never my intention, but I played a part every day. With Daulton and Seth, I played the role of a forty-something man with the extreme good luck of looking far younger than my years. At IU, I played the part of a college freshman. When I traveled, I acted the part of a young, rich heir who spent his life enjoying himself. The last was the nearest to the truth and required little acting. I merely had to conceal my chronological age. It was not difficult. No one would have believed the truth anyway. As for documents, a driver's license, a passport, and such; money could buy almost anything. Yes, my years of studying drama paid off handsomely. I was well prepared for each of the roles that made up my unique life.

Chapter Seventeen: James Black Returns

I walked away from yet another party at the Varsity Villas, somewhat unsteady on my feet. I headed for the stadium parking lot where I'd left my Lotus. I had left it there, hadn't I? I laughed at my own confusion. Perhaps it was best not to drive at all. If I couldn't remember for sure where I'd parked my car I was likely in no condition to drive it. Besides, McNutt wasn't all that far.

I needed to get to bed. I was glad I'd taken care of my needs at the party. I didn't think I was up to taking a boy home. Damn, that sophomore gave great head and didn't hesitate to go down on me even with a couple of girls watching. I bet they got off on seeing us together. The sophomore, whatever his name was, sure knew his business. He made me cum fast. I wasn't sure, but I think he'd typed his number into my phone. If I could remember his name I'd give him a call sometime.

I walked along unsteadily for several minutes then looked around confused. Fuck! I'd been walking toward my apartment instead of my dorm. Worse, I wasn't quite sure where I was. I knew campus well and downtown, but wherever I was it was neither.

I kept walking. I'd come upon something recognizable soon. Bloomington wasn't that big. I'd hit something familiar within a few minutes.

Did I hear footsteps behind me or was I imagining things? I had drank too much. It was the little sophomore's fault. He kept handing me cups, likely in an attempt to get into my pants. It had worked. I shook my head, trying to clear it. From now on I'd be a little more careful. I was old enough to know better after all. I might look eighteen, but I wasn't.

I stumbled. As I righted myself a strong hand clamped over my mouth and an arm wrapped around my chest, pulling me into the shadows. I struggled, but I felt something close around my throat. I grabbed at it in reflex, but it tightened and I gasped for air.

My attacker jerked me around and I saw his face for the first time. It was James Black!

"Thought you'd never see me again, did you?" he said, tightening the noose, for noose it was.

I struggled to answer and to breathe. I could feel my face turning purple. I tried to break free, but James slugged me in the stomach and I doubled over. My vision blacked out, but then I felt the noose loosen. I gasped for air.

"Did you like that? Did you like a little taste of what you did to my brother?"

"You know I'm not him!" I said, trying to think clearly. "You know..."

James rammed his fist into my jaw.

"Oh, you had me fooled. I completely fell for it, but then I got to thinking, and digging. You looked just a little too much like the boy who killed my brother, far too much for coincidence."

"You know I can't be him!"

"You are him. I don't know how it is you haven't changed, but you're him. Perhaps you are the devil himself. I will never forget that face. It's etched in my mind with hatred."

"You're making a mistake! I'm eighteen! I can't be who you think I am! Please! You're making a horrible, horrible mistake!"

"I suppose I'll just have to risk it, won't I? I can probably live with such a mistake. Let me think...yes, I can. If I find out later I killed the wrong guy at least I'll have the pleasure of seeing that face turn purple. I'll have the pleasure of watching you kick and struggle as the noose tightens around your neck. I'll have the pleasure of watching you die, just as my brother died."

"Please!"

"You're asking me for mercy when you had none for my brother?"

"I didn't think he'd kill himself! I was going to him the next day and..."

My hand flew to my mouth, but it was too late. I stared into the eyes of Caleb's brother in sheer horror.

"I knew it," he said.

"Please! I didn't kill him! He killed himself! I didn't mean for him to do it! I loved him! If he had just held on I would have made everything right! I would have..."

James kicked me in the stomach and I doubled over. He dragged me by the rope deeper into the shadows. I grasped for the rope as it tightened around my neck, cutting off my air. James threw the end of the rope over a tree limb. My eyes widened in terror even as I fought to breathe. He was going to hang me.

I managed to loosen the noose enough to breathe. I fought to get it off, but James slugged me in the face. I fell and the noose tightened as it stopped me from hitting the ground. James pulled hard on the other end even as I struggled to dig my fingers behind the rope. If only I could speak I could offer him money, anything and everything, surely there was something, but I couldn't speak. I couldn't breathe. I could feel my face turning purple.

A bright illuminated us as a car sped toward us. It was too bright for a head light. Flashing lights filled the air with strobes of red and blue. Someone had called the cops. I struggled as James desperately hoisted me higher.

"Freeze!"

The commanding voice filled the air, but James didn't freeze. He pulled a handgun from the waist of his jeans and whipped it up toward me. Gunshots filled the air. Seconds later I hit the ground hard. For a few seconds I couldn't see, I couldn't breathe, I couldn't think, then hands that were not mine loosened the noose and pulled it off me. I gasped, drawing in great mouthfuls of oxygen. James lay beside me. Dead.

I began to shake and sob. James had almost hung me. When he ran out of time he tried to gun me down. I'd come so close... I couldn't stop shaking or crying.

"You're going to be all right, son."

I couldn't see through the tears, but I could hear the voice and feel a strong hand on my shoulders. More flashing lights appeared. I was put on a gurney and whisked away in an ambulance. The ride and the emergency room were a blur. I was examined and prodded. I was given something to either calm me down or make me sleep. I woke up later, was told I didn't have any serious injuries, and I could go home if someone would come pick me up. I called Daulton. It was late, but he came. He was horribly distressed when I gave him the barest outline of what had happened, but I reassured him I was okay and that my attacker was dead and no longer a threat.

We were met at the door of McNutt by my R.A. The town police had called the university and alerted them to my location. My R.A. was nearly as worried as Daulton, but I assured him that I was okay. Daulton left me in his hands and he escorted me to my room. I didn't resist. I was shaken to the core, fearful, and still disorientated.

I locked myself in my room, sat down on my bed, and reassured myself that I was okay. James had been brought into the emergency room while I was being treated. He was D.O.A. The police officer had taken him out with two quick shots.

The whole horrible episode probably lasted five minutes at the most. It seemed like forever at the time, but only minutes could have passed between James grabbing me and being gunned down. I had no idea how the cop arrived so fast. I was glad he did. Another minute, two at most, and I would have been dead.

I breathed deeply. I still felt as if I couldn't get enough air. I walked over to the mirror and could see the red marks left by the rope and by my own fingers as I'd clawed at it in desperation. There would be bruises soon, but all that would fade. I knew I was very lucky to be alive.

I tried to sleep, but I kept reliving the horror of the night in my dreams. It started with the footsteps and quickly moved to the noose around my neck. I couldn't breathe as the rope tightened. In the dream, I could see James staring at me and laughing and as I slowly suffocated. That hadn't happened in real life. My vision was so fuzzy I couldn't see anything and my only thought was to breathe. In my dreams, James shifted into Caleb. His dead eyes stared into mine, silently accusing me. Caleb laughed at me as I gasped out my last breath. I always awakened before I died, but no one came to rescue me in my dreams.

I finally did sleep and when I awakened in the morning it took me a while to remember what had happened the night before. I walked to the mirror and examined myself. The evidence of the attack was evident on my neck.

I was lucky to be alive and I knew it. James was a lot stronger than me and with the rope around my neck...I tried to free myself, but I couldn't. I had come very, very close to death.

James said he'd done some digging. Perhaps I hadn't covered my tracks as well as I'd thought or maybe James was unhinged enough to believe the eighteen-year-old I seemed to be was Caleb's boyfriend all those years ago. Maybe my likeness to the Dorian he'd once met was enough. James himself said that if he was wrong he'd still have the pleasure of watching the boy who killed his brother die. I guess it didn't matter. I'd come far too close to death. James was gone now and he couldn't come after me again.

I wasn't looking forward to the attention that was soon to come my way. The attack had probably already made the papers and everyone would be staring at the marks on my neck. The press hadn't hounded me, but then there hadn't been time. At least they couldn't get into McNutt. I had to go to the police station a little later and make a statement. I hoped no one was waiting with a camera there. I didn't want my face in the paper. Physical evidence of my existence could only complicate matters for me, now and in the future.

It was Sunday and I therefore had no classes. It wasn't quite cool enough for a scarf, but I wore one anyway to hide my neck. I drove to the Cracker Barrel for breakfast, mainly because I wasn't likely to see anyone from school there. It was mainly a place for older people and definitely didn't attract the gay crowd.

I had a leisurely breakfast of pancakes with blackberry topping and whipped cream, bacon, and scrambled eggs. When I finished I headed for the Indiana State Police post. I hadn't even noticed the state police the night before, but that's where I was told to go.

I spent a not-so-fun hour and a half answering questions and making a statement. I told the truth, mostly, but of course I left out the real story—that James was the older brother of my dead ex-boyfriend. There was no way that would be an issue.

I spent most of the rest of the day with Daulton. I was right. The story had hit the paper, but luckily included no photo of me. It merely gave my name, age, and noted that I was an IU student. I was sure the Indiana Daily Student would run its own story.

Unfortunately I would be a topic of discussion on campus. At least it was better than being dead.

Daulton fussed over me, but not so much it became an annoyance. I actually kind of liked being pampered. It had been a long time since anyone had taken care of me. I felt safe within his studio as I did not when I walked around Bloomington. Since the attack a sense of ill ease had settled upon me. I knew James was dead and couldn't hurt me but the suddenness and brutality of his attack had unsettled me. I had not expected to see James again. I thought I'd fooled him completely in Dunn's Woods, but some instinct or insanity had caused him to keep digging for the truth. It didn't matter now. Why was I even thinking about it? James was dead.

I sat with a fluted glass of ginger ale, watching as Daulton painted a landscape of Dunn Meadow with the trees and the stream known as the Jordan River just beyond.

"How can you do that?" I asked.

"Do what?" he asked, bringing the leaves of a tree to life with his brushstrokes.

"Paint something that you can't see."

"Oh, I do see it, in my mind. I took my canvas and easel and sketched out the scene at Dunn Meadow. I even did some preliminary painting there. I fixed it all in my mind so I can see the meadow whenever I work on this canvas."

"That is remarkable, Daulton. You have such extraordinary talents. I wish I was half as talented...at anything."

"I'm sure you have some talent hidden away, Dorian. You hardly have the right to complain. You have apparently inexhaustible wealth and lasting youth and beauty. Men would kill to possess any of those things."

Daulton gazed at me and I could tell he was once again wondering how it was that I had shown no signs on aging in all the years I'd known him. He sighed and went back to work on his canvas.

Daulton was nearly sixty now and it showed. He was a good looking man, but he was a good looking man *for his age*. He had aged a quarter of a century in the years I had known him. I had not aged at all.

"Perhaps we all want what we cannot have," I said. "I would give up a good deal of my wealth to be able to paint, or write, or play an instrument."

"I would give much to be young again," Daulton said to me wistfully.

"I bet you would not trade your artistic talent for youth or for any amount of money."

Daulton smiled.

"No. I would not."

"You are the luckier of the two of us then. I have no right to complain, of course, but I am jealous of your talent and continually impressed by it."

Daulton tipped his head to me.

I stiffened when there was a knock at the door and then forced myself to relax. It was ridiculous to be so jumpy. Seth swept into the room.

"I've been trying to find you since I read the paper this morning. Terrible business," Seth said.

Seth pulled me out of my seat and examined my neck.

"You came out of it all right, all things considered," Seth said.

"The marks are already fading," I said.

The marks were fading, far quicker than they should have. I hadn't thought of it until now, but I had no black eye where James had slugged me in the face.

I felt a compulsion to look at the portrait, a compulsion so strong I nearly started for the door, but I forced myself to remain.

"After all these years...James Black. That was Caleb's brother, was it not? You told me about him once, long ago."

"How do you remember these things, Seth? I mentioned meeting him perhaps once, years and years ago, and you still remember the name."

"Caleb's brother?" Daulton asked. "I never made the connection. The man who attacked you was Caleb's brother?"

"Yes. He held me responsible for his brother's death."

I turned away and looked out the window. I could not bear to look in Daulton's eyes for I read there that Daulton held me at least partially responsible for my one-time lover's suicide.

"Ridiculous!" Seth said. "Had Caleb been made of sterner stuff he would still be with us. It is not your fault he was unable to weather the storm."

No one voiced what we all knew, that I was the storm, but Seth was right. I didn't kill Caleb. He killed himself. If only he'd held on we might have been together to this day. I was angry with him for leaving me.

"Are you quite all right, Dorian?" Seth asked.

"The encounter has left me shaken. It was so sudden and unexpected."

"Definitely unexpected. Who would have thought Caleb's brother would appear after so many years?" Seth said.

I shrugged and said nothing about my previous encounter with James.

"From what I read in the paper you had a narrow escape," Seth said.

"Too narrow. I was quite inadequate in my own defense."

"As any of us would be with a rope choking the life out of us," Seth said.

I smiled at him gratefully.

"At least it's all over and done with. James is dead. There are no messy loose ends to trouble you," said Seth.

I nodded.

"I'm sure you're quite tired of discussing it. I know if it happened to me I would want to put it in the past as soon as possible."

"Quite," I said.

"So, are you still seducing unsuspecting college boys with your unnaturally youthful looks? By god, I'd sell my soul to possess your apparently perpetual youth and beauty."

Seth eyed me as if he suspected I had done just that.

"Don't say such things," Daulton said.

"I had one before the attack, although I'd say I allowed him to seduce me. He was eighteen, I think."

"Dorian!" Daulton said.

"Oh, don't sound so shocked or be such a prude, Daulton. The only reason you and I don't land such young men is because we can't. Well, not without paying them anyway."

"Seth!"

"Oh, like there's anything wrong with that, Daulton," said Seth.

"It's illegal."

"Bah! It's commerce. It's an exchange of goods for cash. It's the American way. Poor college boys are always in need of assistance and men of our age are always in need of college boys."

I laughed.

"Speak for yourself," Daulton said.

"I swear you are misplaced in time, Daulton. It's as if you have stepped out of the Victorian age. You really must join the rest of us in the twenty-first century. Perhaps I'll buy you a boy for your birthday," Seth said.

"Don't you dare."

Daulton turned completely scarlet and I had to fight not to laugh.

"Stop tormenting Daulton, Seth."

"Oh, he knows I love him dearly and admire him greatly. He stopped taking anything I say seriously years ago."

"If only others would as well," Daulton said.

"Dorian recognizes my wisdom. Don't you, Dorian?"

I smiled over my glass and took another sip of ginger ale.

Seth and I sat and talked while Daulton painted. It was comfortable sitting there with those two older men. Although I did not see them often, Seth especially, they were still my oldest and closest friends. My life would have been entirely different if I hadn't met them. For one thing, my face would have wrinkles and my hair would have been graying at the temples. Who would have thought that agreeing to pose for a portrait could so utterly change my life?

I remained for some hours, then walked the short distance to my apartment. I stood and stared at my study door. The portrait had been calling out to me, demanding that I look upon it, yet again. A sense of anger emanated from it because I had not come when summoned.

I reluctantly took my key and unlocked the door. I flipped on the lights and removed the black satin cover. I gasped at the malicious, self-satisfied expression on Dorian's face.

Dorian's eyes glared at me, merciless and accusing. They condemned me for another life taken, another life lost because of my actions.

"*He* tried to kill *me*," I said out loud. "I played no part at all in the death of James."

The portrait stood there silently calling me a liar. On that night so many years ago I'd set in motion a chain of events that had killed my lover and now his older brother.

"No! I am not responsible! Caleb killed himself! His brother was mad! He was mad I tell you! Mad!"

I suddenly realized I was shouting at a painting. Dorian gazed at me with an evil smile curling up the corners of his mouth. He was trying to drive me insane. I hated him. I wanted to punch him, but what good would it do to punch a painting and what might it do to me?

I looked at the portrait and ran my fingers over my own cheek. Dorian had a black eye where James had struck me. The red marks on his neck were far more pronounced than those upon my own. I almost took a step back when I noticed them. The rope had left ugly red marks and my own fingers had left scratches where I'd clawed at the rope. There were no scratches upon my own neck and the marks had already faded to almost nothing.

I covered the portrait once more. I could not bear those malicious, accusing eyes. I turned off the lights and locked the room behind me, determined not to gaze upon the painting again for a long, long time.

Chapter Eighteen: Dorian Gray Unmasked

I returned to class on Monday. The physical evidence of the attack was, thankfully, gone. Still, those who knew my name, and there were many, gawked at me as I passed. Many offered their support. I was touched by their compassion. People who barely knew me actually cared about what happened to me. Some were likely ingratiating themselves because they wanted to get into my pants, but even straight boys and girls who knew I was gay showed sympathy.

The attention was not too hard to bear. I think it would have been worse if the rope burns and claw marks were still upon my neck and the my eye was blackened. I did not look like a victim.

I crossed Evan's path, but he did not look at me. No doubt he wished me dead. If James had succeed, Evan would have been rid of me. I was still alive and I was not finished with Evan. I could not kept him captive forever, but he was too gorgeous to free.

I checked the time on my smart phone. I didn't have much time to spare, but I needed some distraction and some relief. I texted Evan and told him to meet me by the third floor restroom in the Simon Music Library and Recital Hall on the corner of 3rd Street and Jordan Avenue.

I received a text in seconds telling me he was on his way. I knew he would do what he was told. He knew what would happen if he didn't.

I spotted Evan crossing Jordan just up ahead of me as I walked toward our rendezvous. I'd chosen our place of meeting because it was quiet and little used. There would be little chance of us being disturbed there. It was also close to my next destination.

Evan spotted me as I walked toward the restroom. I nodded with my head for him to follow me and led him into the last stall. Evan looked around nervously as I closed and locked the door.

"Here?" he whispered, looking frightened.

For answer, I grabbed his shoulder and shoved him to his knees. He knew what was expected of him and got to work. I closed my eyes and enjoyed the sensation. Sex was truly one of the great joys of life and forcing a straight boy to blow me made it ever hotter.

I opened my eyes, looked down, and watched Evan. I grinned. I grasped both sides of his head and thrust into his mouth, making him take me deeper and deeper. He gagged and choked.

I pushed him off, pulled him to his feet, and unfastened his belt. I popped the button on his jeans, ripped down the zipper, and shoved his jeans and boxer-briefs to the floor. I turned him around and shoved him up against the wall. I pressed myself against his firm, tight ass.

"No, man! Please! I'm begging you!" Evan pleaded in a loud whisper.

I rammed myself deep inside him and he cried out in pain. This is what I wanted to do to James Black for attacking me. I wanted to make him pay. I shoved myself all the way into Evan and smiled when I heard him begin to cry.

I ran my hands up under Evan's shirt and groped his muscular pecs as I thrust into him. I wrapped one arm around his chest and pulled myself against him as I used him. I pounded myself into him harder and harder as he whimpered and groaned in pain. The sounds of his humiliated sobs filled the stall.

I wanted to keep on using him, but I was far too aroused. I moaned loudly and lost control. I bred Evan's straight, tight ass.

When I'd finished. I pulled out and stuffed myself back into my boxer-briefs and jeans. I walked out into the restroom to find a nervous looking but cute college boy just finishing up at a urinal. I grinned at him and washed my hands.

The boy kept looked me as he joined me by the sinks. He had a sizable bulge in his jeans. It gave me an idea. I leaned over and whispered to him. His face paled, but then he nodded. I lead him back to the stall. Evan had dressed, but was sitting on the toilet. He looked up surprised when I pushed the door open with a boy standing beside me.

"Blow him," I said.

Evan looked at me incredulously and shook his head.

"Do it now, bitch," I said in a menacing tone.

Evan shot me a look of pure hatred, but grabbed the boy's zipper and pulled it down. I stood there and watched as Evan gave a complete stranger head. Forcing him to serve another college boy was an exquisite humiliation. I almost enjoying watching as much as I'd enjoyed using Evan in the stall myself.

I watched until the boy moaned and then pulled back. I couldn't help but laugh at Evan.

"You might want to leave before anyone else comes in," I said, hinting that I'd make him blow them too.

Evan's face paled. He looked like he wanted to say something nasty, but then thought better of it. He was right. I wasn't in the mood to put up with any crap from him. Evan was out the door in moments. I smiled at the boy, then departed as well.

James had tried to take my life, but he had failed. My close brush with death had reminded me that I had to make the most of every single day. I did not age, but I realized now death could and would someday come for me. I had to fill each day with pleasure and new experiences as if it was my last. I laughed out loud as I walked outside. I had certainly done so today. Poor Evan. If he knew what was coming...if he knew the plans I was even now making for him...he'd hang himself like Caleb just to escape.

***

Daulton called and asked to see me in the evening, which was unusual indeed. I wasn't quite in the mood for him, but when he told me he was departing that very night for Paris and did not know when he would return I thought I had best see him. He wished for me to look in on his studio while he was away. Daulton had done much for me, so I could hardly say no. Well, I could have, but Daulton was one of the two real friends I had in my life. I told him to meet me at my apartment in The Kirkwood at 8 p.m.

Daulton seemed unaccountably nervous as he sat upon the couch in my living room. He refused my offer of coffee or tea. He kept opening his mouth as if about to speak, but then closed it again. I was beginning to lose patience with him. This was not the evening I'd planned.

"Tell me what is on your mind, Daulton," I said at last.

"Please don't be angry with me, Dorian, but...I was wondering if I might take the portrait with me to Paris..."

"That's completely out of the question. I'm surprised you even desire to do so. You've said more than once you put far too much of yourself into it to exhibit it."

"I did say that, yes, but...it is the best work I've ever done and there's a chance...a small chance but a chance still that I might get to exhibit a painting in the Louvre. It's a rare, rare opportunity, but it could seal my standing as a great artist. Please, Dorian. I hate to ask, but..."

I shook my head.

"If it was any other painting of yours in my collection..."

"None of the others even comes close. You know that, Dorian. The portrait I painted of you all those years ago was my masterpiece. I have tried, believe me, but I have never been able to surpass or even equal it."

"I'm afraid it's impossible, Daulton."

"Why, Dorian? This means so much to me. You haven't even allowed me to look upon my own work for all these years."

"I...can't explain."

"It wasn't stolen, was it? Destroyed? Sold?"

I was tempted to lie and tell Daulton it had been stolen, but something would not allow me.

"No. It is quite safe."

"Please, Dorian. Let me at least see it. Perhaps it is not the masterpiece I remember it to be. If I can see it and know that, I will not trouble you about it again."

"No, Daulton."

"Please, Dorian. I do not ask for much from you..."

"You ask very much now!"

"Why is it so much to ask? If it is exhibited, it will be in Paris. Your name need not be mentioned. It is very unlikely anyone here will know. I'd like to tell Seth, of course, but you know you can count on his discretion."

"It simply is too much to ask. You must accept that answer."

"I can't! Why do you keep it hidden from everyone and from me? It was my greatest work of art and it has remained unseen! Only Seth has viewed it and only once before you hid it away!"

Daulton was being quite tiresome and I was growing increasingly irritated with him by the moment.

"Do you really want it see, Daulton? Do you?" I asked angrily. "Do you *truly* want to know why I let no one see it? Haven't you ever wondered why I do not age, Daulton?"

"You are...one of the lucky few who..."

"You know it's more than that. You suspect it or you know it. It's the painting, Daulton! The painting ages for me and more than that. It bears my sins."

Daulton looked at me in horror.

"Dorian, you are unwell..."

"Mad you mean! You think I'm insane, don't you? Do you want me to prove it to you? Do you want me to show you what has become of your masterpiece? You will be very sorry if I do, I assure you, *very* sorry."

"I must see it, for your sake as much as mine," Daulton said gravely.

My old friend did believe I had gone insane, and why not? The words I was speaking were insane, or would be if they were not true. Perhaps I *was* insane. The painting had been speaking to me, not with words, but speaking to me none-the-less. I had often wondered myself if I was mad. How could a portrait bear my age and sin? It was ludicrous. Perhaps when Daulton saw the painting he would see exactly what he'd seen on the day he finished it. Then, I would know I was mad. If not...

"Very well."

I led Daulton to the study door. I unlocked it, flipped on the lights, and Daulton stepped inside.

I pulled off the black stain cover and Daulton recoiled in horror. I knew he was seeing exactly what I did. He looked at me and back to the painting.

"This is monstrous!"

"This is me," I said.

"No. I did not paint this! Where is the portrait, Dorian? Why have you played this cruel joke on me?"

"It's no joke, Daulton. Remember the conversation we had the day you finished the painting? Remember how Seth told me that the only things that really mattered in life were youth and beauty? When I looked upon my portrait, I was jealous of it, for that Dorian would never age. I knew that even in those moments I stood there I had grown older. I wished that the portrait would age instead of me and my wish came true. I don't know how, but it came true. Not only does the portrait age for me, it bears all my sins. You see in the portrait the real me."

Daulton shook his head.

"Look at me, my old friend. Look at my face."

Daulton did so.

"I have not aged since the day you finished that portrait. I do not age slowly. I am not young-looking. I have aged not at all and I am young. I should be in my forties, but I am not. I am eighteen. Look at me! Can you deny it? Can you deny that I have not changed in all the long years?"

Daulton looked away and then back at me. He put his hand over his mouth, then removed it. He stared at me with wide eyes.

"How?" he asked.

"I told you."

"That cannot be."

"It is."

Daulton looked at the portrait. I could read the revulsion on his face, not at the wear and tear of years, but at the cruel eyes and upturned mouth, at the lustful, hateful sneer.

"That cannot be you. If sin is truly etched upon a man's features then this creature...this creature has done unspeakable things."

"I have done unspeakable things, Daulton."

He shook his head.

"Shall I tell you what I did just today? Shall I tell you about the college boy I raped? The list of my crimes and depravities is long, but that one may stand in for all."

Daulton looked at me in horror and disgust. He kept looking from the portrait back to me as if only then realizing what he was seeing.

"I don't even know you," he said quietly and without friendship or love.

"No, you don't."

"I cannot allow this to continue. I gave you this painting but now I take it back. It must be destroyed and if you are destroyed along with it, so much the better."

Daulton moved to pull the painting from its easel. I grabbed his shoulder and we struggled. My heel caught on a display case and I fell. Daulton grasped the painting. He was doing to destroy it!

I scrambled to my feet, grabbed a dagger from the display on the wall, and rushed him. He knew the truth now. He could not live.

We tumbled to the floor. Daulton struggled against me, but I was the stronger. In moments he was on his back, his eyes filled with tears and terror. I drew back the dagger, but my arm froze, trembling. I was in a murderous rage. I wanted to kill him. I had to kill him, but he had been one of my only friends. How evil had I become that I could do this?

I threw the dagger to the corner of the room, climbed off Daulton, sat upon the floor, and sobbed.

"It's true! I should be destroyed! I have done such horrible, unthinkable things! I killed Caleb! I drove him to kill himself and so I killed him! His brother's blood is on my hands too! I have blackmailed and raped and murdered. I have taken delight in cruelty. Do the world and me a favor and destroy the painting! If I am not destroyed along with it then take the dagger I would have used to murder you, my best friend, and plunge it into my heart."

My sobs became uncontrollable as the weight of my of guilt and sin fell upon me. Seeing my own evil in the painting wasn't enough. Seeing it in Daulton's eyes wasn't either. Nearly murdering one who had been nothing but kind to me had showed me what I really was. I could not endure it.

My sobs quieted and I became aware that Daulton had not moved. He looked upon me with pity.

"Destroy it," I said.

Daulton shook his head.

"Then I will."

I stood and moved toward the dagger.

"Dorian, no!"

Daulton gripped my shoulder and forced me to look at him.

"One who displays such remorse cannot be all bad. If there was no good in you, you would have killed me. I have known a kind and loving boy for many years. I witnessed his happiness when he found his one, true love. I witnessed his sorrow when his love took his own life. You tried to hide your pain, but I saw it. That sorrow has never left you in all these years. I see that boy still when I look at you. I cannot allow you to destroy the painting or yourself while there is yet hope and there is always hope, Dorian! Always!"

"It's too late!"

"Trust my judgment, Dorian. Trust one who loves you and has since the first moment he saw you. It is never too late. Can't you see? The change is already beginning, here and now! Do not take my friend from me, for if you do that you will be committing a great evil. I have asked little of you, but I ask this of you now. Take the more difficult path. Live. Perhaps you can erase the sins painted on this canvas. Nothing can take the years away, but you can take away the sins. Be the Dorian I always knew you could be."

I broke down and cried in Daulton's arms, horrible wails that echoed the pain in my heart. He held me and it felt almost as if I had a father again. Daulton had long been more father to me than mine had ever been. He held me as I cried for many long minutes. At last, after how long I do not know, I pulled back, wiped my eyes, and nodded.

Daulton and I looked at the portrait together. I trembled, but Daulton put his arm over my shoulder.

"Do you really think I can undo what I've done?" I asked in a timid voice that did not sound like my own.

"No one can undo what has been done, Dorian, but you can make amends where possible and you can change your life. There is much good in you, Dorian, let that good rule your life."

Dorian stared at us balefully from the frame. He gazed at us both with pure hatred and contempt. He whispered in my mind that I was too weak to change—that I would fail no matter how hard I tried. I refused to listen to him. I would succeed because I must. If I could not change I had no choice but to destroy the portrait and thereby myself. Perhaps such destruction was just, but what would it do to Daulton? Destroying myself would only add to the heap of my sins.

Daulton helped me cover the portrait once more. We left the study and I locked the door behind us.

"I think I shall put off my trip," Daulton said.

"No. You cannot pass up this opportunity. You are a great artist, Daulton. Take your finest paintings and I am sure at least one of them will be judged worthy. Besides, what artist can resist Paris?"

"You might need me."

"I *will* need you, but that is what phones are for, Daulton. I will call you. While you are gone I will strive to be the Dorian you think I can be. When you return, I hope you will find a much better man than you left."

I hugged Daulton.

"You look tired," Daulton said.

"I am. I shall go to bed soon."

"Will you be okay?"

I nodded.

"I'll leave you then. Call me whenever you need me."

Daulton turned to go.

"Daulton?"

"Yes?" he said, turning back.

"Thank you."

I leaned in and gave him a chaste kiss upon the lips. He smiled.

"Good night, Dorian."

"Good night."

I stood there in my living room for a few moments. I gazed at the study door. I could feel Dorian in there. I could almost hear him laughing at me. I would not let him unnerve me. I knew what I had to do and I would do it.

The portrait had been a mirror for the ugliness of my soul almost since the moment of its creation. When I discovered that the portrait bore the evidence of my sins, I fooled myself into believing that it bore the sins themselves. I knew now that was not true. I'd known it for some time but would not acknowledge it. Coming so very close to murdering Daulton forced me to truly see myself in that portrait. I had been doing whatever I wanted with no thought for others. I thought of Evan and nearly became ill. He was where I had to start.

I moved to my computer and set to work. It did not take long. Soon, all evidence of Evan was gone—the website, the videos, and photos, all of it. As soon as that was accomplished I called him and asked him to meet me at my dorm room. I locked up the apartment, hopped in my Lotus and drove to McNutt.

Evan arrived shortly after I did. He gazed at me fearfully but resigned to his fate. How much damage had I done to this teenage boy?

"Have a seat," I said.

Evan did as he was told.

"Something happened to me tonight," I said. "I received a wake-up call. I almost did something...but there is no need to speak of that. I have been horribly cruel to you. I have ill-used you in unspeakable ways. I asked you here to tell you that it's over."

"You not going to release the address of the website, are you?" Evan asked, obviously terrified at the thought.

"No. There is no website anymore. I destroyed it. I erased every video and every photo of you. Well, I did keep one photo of you, fully-clothed, as a reminder of the horrible things I have done to you."

"I don't understand."

"Your nightmare is over, Evan. I will never trouble you again. I am so very sorry for what I've done to you. No one deserves to be so horribly used and especially one who never did me any wrong. I took advantage of your lust for a girl to lure you in and trap you. Then I used you mercilessly to satisfy my own lust. I am truly ashamed of that now. I do not ask for your forgiveness for how could you forgive such a horror? I am truly sorry and I will prove that by never bothering you again."

Evan looked at me as if he did not believe me.

"I am sincere. You have the website address and the password. Check it now," I said, indicating the laptop on my desk.

Evan did so and looked back at me when he saw that it was gone.

"I do not expect you to trust me, but it's all gone, Evan. You are safe from me now."

Evan gazed at me with pained eyes. He was on the verge of tears.

"Why did you do this to me?" he asked.

"Because you are handsome, built, and straight, but most of all because I could. I did not have a conscience to stop me. I did not have the strength to resist. Now, I do. I know there is nothing I can do to make things right, but I will not go on abusing you. I am truly sorry."

Evan just looked at me.

"I want you to have something, but I want you to understand that I am not trying to buy your forgiveness. I do not expect you to forgive me—ever. I am also not trying to ease my own conscience, because nothing can erase what I have done. I will regret what I did to you forever. I will always look upon it with shame. I cannot give you back what I've taken from you, but I want you to have this."

I handed him a set of keys. He looked at me with a question in his eyes.

"I want you to have my Lotus. I will have the title transferred to you immediately and I will set up an account to pay for the license and insurance for as long as you own the car. I will also have a gas card delivered to you that will automatically be refilled so you will never have to purchase gas."

"How can you afford this?" Evan asked, incredulously.

"Believe me, I can and easily. I know this doesn't make up for what I did to you, but I know straight boys love cars so...at least you get something."

Evan gazed at me long and hard.

"You are serious. Aren't you?"

I nodded.

"It's really over?"

"Yes."

Evan released a huge breath. I could almost see the huge weight I'd placed upon his shoulders fall away.

I walked him toward the door.

"Have a good night, Evan."

He gazed at me, dazed, but then opened the door and departed. I had done such horrible things to that boy. The true horror of it was that I could never take away the pain and humiliation of it. I was a truly evil creature. No. I *had been* a truly evil creature. I would be no longer.

I undressed, slipped into bed, and fell quickly asleep.

Chapter Nineteen: Making Amends

I skipped my classes the next morning, walked over to Enterprise on North Walnut, and rented a car. I spent the morning arranging all the details of giving the Lotus to Evan, had a quick lunch at the Pita Pit on Indiana Avenue, and then drove around town looking at cars. I couldn't find anything I liked, so I headed for Indianapolis. There I fell in love with a loaded, red 2011 BMW Z4 convertible. After minor haggling, I wrote out a check, and was promised delivery the next day. I drove back to Bloomington in my rental, excited about my new car. It cost about $20,000 less than the Lotus, but it was sporty and I wanted something a little less ostentatious.

I made a few stops in Bloomington, picking up insurance cards and such, then called Evan and asked where he'd like to meet me. He selected the neutral turf of the lobby of the Biddle Hotel in the Memorial Union. I met him there half an hour later and handed over the title to the Lotus, the insurance documents and cards, the gas card, and everything else he would need.

"I half expected to get picked up by the cops for driving a stolen car," Evan said.

"I don't blame you, but time will show you I am sincere."

Evan nodded.

"Once again, I'm sorry. Goodbye."

I walked away without looking back. I could never set things right with Evan, but I had stopped abusing him and had tried to offset what I'd done to him a little. It was a beginning on my new life and I felt good about that at least.

My next stop was the police station to gather some details. I obtained the name of the officer who had saved me and left my phone number with a request for him to call. Then, I parked my rental at the stadium, walked to McNutt, changed, and walked to the SRSC for a workout. I needed something to get my mind off the turmoil of the last twenty-four hours.

There were some hot guys working out, more than one of whom checked me out, but I wasn't in the mood to hook up. I had no intention of giving up sex. There was nothing wrong with sex, if all those involved were willing. My memories of my sexual encounters with Evan haunted me, especially the final when I'd used him in a restroom stall and purposely hurt him.   I wasn't quite ready to have sex again.

My cell rang at the end of my workout. It was Gene Florence, the officer who had saved my life. I arranged to meet him at Bucceto's. I showered at the SRSC, enjoying the view of the two hunky college boys who were showering just then too. I dressed then walked to the stadium where I'd left my rental car.

I made it to Bucceto's with five minutes to spare. Officer Gene Florence was reasonably handsome with dark hair and eyes. He had a firm handshake which I'd expected. I'd met him on the night of the attack and had seen him when I was giving my statement, but I was too shaken then to pay much attention.

"Thank you for coming," I said. "I wanted to express my appreciation for what you did for me in a tangible way."

"That's not necessary."

"It is to me. If you hadn't acted so quickly I'd be dead now. For starters I'm paying for supper. Please order whatever you like. No arguments," I said with a grin.

"I surrender," Gene said. I liked his sense of humor.

We talked as we browsed the menus. We had just met so we talked about Bloomington, the one thing we had in common other than the events of the night James almost killed me.   I learned that Gene was married and had a young son. I told him I was a college student, but he already knew that. We got on well for strangers.

When our waiter came Gene ordered rosemary cream chicken and I ordered shrimp Santa Cruz. Our dinners came with salad and garlic bread.

We talked a bit about what I was studying and about Gene's son. He was quite proud of him. We discussed the general lack of serious crime in Bloomington, with the notable except of the attack I survived. Soon, our food arrived and we talked a good deal less. The food at Bucceto's deserves special attention.

"I would like to do more than just buy you supper to express my gratitude," I said when we'd finished eating.

"That's completely unnecessary. I was just doing my job. I am a police officer."

"I think it's necessary," I said, taking out my checkbook.

"It's really not, please. I would not feel right about accepting anything from you. I don't even know if I would consider it ethical."

"It's not like I'm trying to influence you or buy my way out of a parking ticket," I said as I wrote out a check. "I was the victim, not the perpetrator. There is no conflict of interest here. It's merely me expressing my appreciation for you saving my life. I am in a position to be tangibly grateful. I'm sure you aren't paid nearly enough. I don't see how you could possibly be paid enough to put your life on the line like you do. I absolutely insist you accept this."

I slid the check across the table. Gene looked at it then back up at me, astonished.

"I assure you I am quite serious," I said. "I am *very* well off."

"I...I...simply cannot accept this. I..."

"I'm sure you're going to want your son to attend IU someday. Tuition gets more expensive by the year. If you won't accept my check for yourself, accept it for him."

"But...this check is for half a million dollars."

"I know. I wrote it," I said, grinning.

"I... You..."

I kept grinning. I enjoyed watching Gene's disconcertment, but my real pleasure came from my ability to reward someone who truly deserved it in a way he likely never dreamed possible. It was a far more satisfying joy than the sadistic pleasure I had derived from using a straight boy in unspeakable ways. This pleasure would leave me with no guilt, but instead with a sense of having done right.

"I have an enormous fortune and money comes in faster than I can spend it. I intend to give to many charities, but first I wish to reward someone who has truly earned it. I know you didn't save me with any thought of reward. Just as you don't go out and do you job every day with any thought of reward beyond the knowledge that you are helping and protecting others. I'm sure this check pales in comparison to the satisfaction your career brings to you, but I also know that no one who serves the public is paid even close to what they are worth. Please accept this. You have earned it, not just by saving me, but for all you have done and for dedicating yourself to others. It will make me very happy if you will accept it. In fact, I absolutely insist and I always get what I want."

Gene was still speechless.

"I...I don't know what to say. Thank you."

"No, thank you," I said. "All that I ask is that you keep this quiet, or rather that you keep my name out of it."

"Of course," Gene said.

The waiter came with our check. I paid and left him a very large tip. I found that I enjoyed being generous. Gene and I walked out together.

"Thank you again for saving my life," I said. "I am forever in your debt."

Poor Gene was still quite flustered, which made me smile. Here was a man with the courage to put his life at risk every day, but he didn't quite know how to react to good fortune. We bid each other goodbye and I walked to my rental car and drove it back to the stadium parking lot. From there, I walked the short distance to McNutt. I was happier than I had been in a long time.

Once in my dorm room, I settled into being a college boy. I had skipped my classes for the day, which I guess only made me that much more a typical college student. I still had work to do and I tackled it instead of running out to a party. I had no intention of giving up parties, but I'd had quite enough excitement for the day. I kept picturing the expression on Gene's face when I'd handed him a check for half a million dollars. Who would have ever thought that giving away money could be so much fun? I worked away until late and then turned in.

I did not awaken until the next morning when my alarm sounded. I got up, slipped my wrap-a-round around my waist and walked to the showers. I was treated to the sight of the bare ass of a college boy as he was drying off. There was definitely an advantage to using a communal shower. I pulled off my wrap, hung it and my towel on a hook, and stepped into the shower.

I loved the luxurious warmth of the water as it cascaded down over my smooth, muscled body. Gabrial Diaddio had taught me all about keeping in shape long ago. I wondered where he was now. I wondered too about the one who got away—Brendan. Was he still with his boyfriend? It was probably a good thing I never got my hands on Brendan. Who knows what harm I would have done? My relationship with Gabrial had worked out fine, but then he was so incredibly gorgeous and built I couldn't wrap him around my little finger like I had so many others.

I ran my soapy hands down over my smooth, taut torso. I was glad I'd kept myself in shape. I was no muscle boy, but I'd never wanted that. I just wanted to be toned with a nicely, but not overly muscled body. I had succeeded.

I rinsed off, stepped out of the stall, and grabbed my towel. I smiled to myself when I noticed a boy checking me out when he thought I could not see him. I took my time drying my hair so he could get a good look, then turned around and dried my front so he could check out my ass. I slipped on my wrap and smiled at him as I left the restroom.

I drew more than the usual amount of attention as I attended my morning classes. So much had happened since the attack it seemed like a distant event. All that had happened with Daulton had pushed the events of the night I was nearly murdered to the side. Every time I thought about what I had almost done to Daulton I was filled with shame. That led to remorse for all the other horrible things I'd done in my life. I had been a bully, and a sadistic one at that. Bully wasn't nearly a strong enough word for it. I did not often use physical strength to push others around, but I had bullied others in far more insidious ways. I shuddered and reminded myself that I was trying to change. I had taken the first step when I had released Evan from his captivity.

I enjoyed my classes and deflected as much attention as I could. I never minded the attention I receive for my looks, but I didn't like to be the object of curiosity. It seemed as if everyone was talking about the attack and there were times I felt like hiding. Even the sympathy looks became annoying. In classes I could largely forget about all that and concentrate on the lecture or discussion. I enjoyed my classes and smiled with the knowledge that I could be a college student forever if I wished.

During my biggest break between classes I took a campus bus to the stadium and returned my rental car. I walked back to the stadium and waited. Right on time, my new BMW convertible rolled in. The salesman got out and handed me the keys, then rode away with his ride back to the dealership.

I climbed behind the wheel. I couldn't wait to drive my new car, but I wasn't finished with classes. I took a last whiff of new-car smell, closed and locked the door, then caught a campus bus back to the main part of campus.

I experience more of the same unwanted attention, but I put on my aloof demeanor and that discouraged most from approaching me. I immersed myself in my classes once again and had a rather agreeable day.

After classes, I ran across the little sophomore who had seduced me with beer at the party before my attack. He headed directly toward me the moment he spotted me. No doubt he wanted more of what he'd had the night. I sometimes had a problem with hookups approaching me in public. They seemed to think that having sex with me once gave them a claim on me.

"Are you okay? I've been so worried about you. They wouldn't let me ride in the ambulance and wouldn't tell me anything in the emergency room since I'm not family."

I was stunned into silence for a moment.

"You were there?"

"Yes, I...well, I was stalking you. I wanted to find out where you lived and I had gotten you rather drunk so I wanted to make sure you got home all right. Then, that horrible man attacked you. I called 911 and..."

"That's how the cop got there so fast," I said.

"I wanted to help, but the dispatcher told me to stay back. I couldn't stand it after a bit and started to rush forward, but that's when the patrol car showed up."

"I'd be dead now if you hadn't been there," I said, staring at him. "I'm sorry. I don't remember your name."

"I never told you. I'm Trace. Trace Canterville."

"Well, Trace Canterville, thank you for saving my life. I thought I had only a police officer to thank, but now there is also you."

Trace blushed.

"I just called 911."

"Which allowed that town cop to arrive just in time to keep me from being killed."

"I should have done more."

"He had a gun, Trace. He would have killed you. I owe you."

Trace blushed again. He was cuter than I'd realized in my drunken haze the night of the party. No matter what he looked like, he was another I owed big. This little gay boy had just hit the jackpot.

"What are you doing now?" I asked.

"I'm done with classes, so studying is my big exciting plan."

"Why don't you put that off for a while and let me take you out to dinner? Then, we can go to my place and I'll show you just how grateful I am."

I swear I could see Trace's dick growing in his pants as I spoke.

"I'd like that a lot," he said, his voice husky with desire.

Trace rode with me on a campus bus to the stadium where I led Trace to my BMW. His eyes widened when I unlocked the passenger door for him.

"Wow, this is one incredible car!"

"I just got it today. I haven't even had the chance to drive it yet," I said. "Hmm, what's your favorite food?"

"Italian."

"DeAngelo's then, I think. Have you ever been there?"

"No, it's a bit out of my range. I'm a Fazoli's boy."

"There's nothing wrong with Fazoli's, but you'll love DeAngelo's and you must promise me to order whatever you want. It's all on me. As I said, I owe you."

There was that blush again. I leaned over and kissed Trace on the lips. He grinned.

I started up the BMW and headed for the DeAngelo's on the eastside near the mall.

In only minutes we were seated at a booth inside the upscale Italian restaurant. We browsed the menu.

"Oh, the Sicilian Calzone sounds good," Trace said.

"Order it then. Order anything and everything you want. You saved my life and I value my life *very* highly."

"You don't have to do anything for me. I just didn't want you to get hurt. I just did what anyone should have done."

"Maybe so, but the point is you did it and I'm alive because of it. So, order any and everything you want!"

I laughed.

"Yes, sir! I wouldn't want to get beaten up for not ordering enough."

When our waiter came, a very sexy blond boy of our age, Trace ordered his calzone and a Coke. I ordered Creole Seafood Cannelloni and a Coke. I had never ordered the Creole Cannelloni before, but it sounded great—seasoned shrimp and crawfish blended with homemade ricotta, smoked mozzarella and asiago cheeses rolled in a pasta shell smothered with Brandy cream sauce, served with marinara. I couldn't wait to try it.

Frank Sinatra, Perry Como, and Louie Armstrong played softly in the background as we sat in our booth. The music fit perfectly with the Italian décor and created a mellow mood.

"I can't believe I'm here with you," Trace said. "I can't believe we hooked up."

"I can't believe someone tried to kill me."

"He must have been some kind of psycho. Who waits in the shadows with a noose?"

"Yeah, he was a psycho, but let's talk about something else. I know I brought it up, but I'd just as soon forget."

"Okay, let's go back to I can't believe we hooked up." Trace grinned.

"Well, you did get me drunk or very nearly."

"I find it a useful tool for getting what I want."

"Me too."

"I can't believe anyone would turn you down."

"Straight guys do."

"Wow, you've hooked up with straight boys? You are a *god*!"

"Yes, I have." I thought of Evan for a moment and guilt assailed me, but I pushed him out of my mind. I was determined to be that Dorian no more.

"I was afraid to approach you. You're so incredibly good looking and so aloof."

"Aloof?" I asked.

"I don't mean unfriendly exactly, just...out of reach."

"You reached me pretty well. You give incredible head by the way, maybe the best I've ever had."

"Well, if you want some more..."

"I do. I intend to pay you back in ways you will truly appreciate. I know what gay boys like. I am one, after all."

"Dorian, you just made me hard as a rock," Trace said quietly.

"Good, you'll be needing that later."

Trace looked completely overwhelmed; as if he'd just won the lottery or entered Heaven. I felt good about myself just then. I didn't often think of others, but I intended to show Trace a very good time. I would enjoy it as well, but our time together was about him. It wouldn't be just tonight either. I intended to give this cute little college boy unprecedented access to my body. If it wasn't for him, my body would already be rotting away so it seemed only fair.

"What's that music playing?" Trace asked as we ate.

"Big band. It was popular in the 1940s. Glenn Miller and Benny Goodman were a couple of the biggest artists back then."

"I've never heard of them."

"Wow, you are young."

Trace just looked at me.

"I'm a year older than you, Dorian. You're eighteen, right?"

I laughed off my mistake.

"Yeah. I should have said you're like most young guys. You don't listen to oldies."

"I don't think that's why you said it."

I stiffened for a moment.

"I'm small, so most people think I'm younger than I am."

I relaxed.

"You could pass for sixteen. You *are* a college student, right? I didn't let some underage high school boy suck me off, did I?" I grinned.

"No."

"You do look young, but you're very sexy, Trace."

He smiled.

"One of the things I like about DeAngelo's is the music," I continued. "It's different. Sitting here you might hear Tony Bennet, Perry Como or Nate King Cole, or Bing Crosby. You don't hear that kind of music anywhere else."

"I've heard of Bing Crosby," Trace said.

"Let me guess—*White Christmas*, right?"

"Yeah," Trace said and laughed.

We had a wonderful meal. The food was incredible and I found I rather liked Trace. I'd forgotten about him at the party almost as soon as my orgasm ended, but I was glad to be with him now. I did not like the circumstance that had brought us together, but if I had a second person to repay for saving my life I'm glad it was a cute boy who was orally talented.

After our meal I took Trace back to my apartment, giving him the story that it belonged to my parents. I fixed him a drink and sat with him on the couch. We began to make out and I discovered Trace was as good at making out as he was at giving head.

When we'd made out a good long time and gotten ourselves rather worked up, I stood and undressed. I stripped completely naked in front of Trace.

"Here is your reward. You can do anything with me or to me that you desire."

Trace nearly panted at the sight of my body and at my words. He stood up, pulled me to him, and kissed me deeply. He nibbled on my earlobes and neck. He licked all over my torso and fell to his knees. Once again, I experienced his superior skill at giving head. This time I wasn't inebriated and enjoyed it even more. Trace took his time, brought me nearly to the edge, then licked his way up over my abdomen and chest again.

It was time to give Trace some enjoyment of another kind. I stripped him naked and licked over his torso as he had mine. When his breath grew ragged, I gently pushed him back in a chair, kneeled down in front of him, and pulled his cock into my mouth. I didn't have the talent Trace did, but I made him moan.

"I can't believe you're blowing me," Trace said.

"Tonight, I'll do anything you want," I said and went back to giving him as much pleasure as I could manage.

I continued working on Trace until he pushed me away. He gazed at me with lust-filled eyes.

"Can I fuck you?"

"You don't have to ask," I said and grinned. "Tonight, I'm yours to do with as you please."

I led Trace into my bedroom by the hand, pulled a condom out of a drawer, and handed it to him. He was so worked up he had trouble rolling it on. He pushed me onto my back on the bed, lifted my legs over his shoulders, and entered me. A look of pure joy crossed his sexy-cute features.

We gazed into each other's eyes as Trace thrust into me. He varied his pace, sometimes using long, slow, deep thrusts and sometimes stabbing his cock into me with lightning speed. His whimpers and moans turned me on almost as much as the sensation of being penetrated by this cute, sexy college boy.

I didn't expect Trace to last long. His wild moans and groans and his frantic thrusts made it seem as if he was on the edge of an intense orgasm, but he didn't lose control. He kept pounding himself into me until sweat ran down his smooth, slim torso. He made me moan, groan, and whimper with delight.

After thirty minutes, Trace was still going. I was a writhing mass of pleasure by then. I arched my back, moaned loudly, and shot my load all over my tight torso. Trace went at me harder and faster than ever and in a few moments he buried himself instead me and howled in ecstasy.

When he finished, he collapsed on top of me, gasping for breath.

"You are a stud," I said and meant.

"You are just so fucking gorgeous."

Trace kissed me deeply and kept on kissing me. I surrendered myself to him completely.

Later, we showered together at Trace's request. Then, I did something I had not done for a very, very long time. I asked him if he wanted to spend the night. We climbed into my bed. I lay on my side. Traced snuggled up against me, pressing his naked body into my backside. Soon, we both fell asleep.

The next morning, I lay there dreaming about someone giving me head. I awakened and found it was no dream. Trace had pulled the covers down and was expertly going down on me. When he saw that I had awakened, he walked over to the drawer where I kept my condoms, pulled one out, walked back to the bed and unrolled it over my hard cock. He straddled me and lowered himself onto me. I moaned as I felt myself sliding in. Trace was incredibly tight.

He began to ride me and the very sight of him bouncing up and down, impaling himself upon me, was almost enough to make me shoot. Trace began to stroke himself in time with his downward thrusts. The sights and sounds were too much for me and I knew I couldn't maintain control much longer. Trace forced himself all the way down on my cock, moaned and exploded all over my chest and neck. That sent me over the edge and I moaned as my orgasm spread through my entire body.

When we had both finished, Trace leaned over and kissed me on the lips.

"Good morning," he said.

"Good morning indeed."

Trace laughed, took my hand, and pulled me into the bathroom for another shower.

After we dried off and dressed, I took Trace to the Runcible Spoon for breakfast. It was one of the first spring days warm enough to eat al fresco so I thought we should take advantage.

The Runcible Spoon was the same place I'd taken Caleb all those years ago. My mind was on the present instead of the past at the moment. Trace was grinning from ear to ear.

"That was THE night of my life," he said as we sat at an outdoor table among the trees and plants.

"That was the idea and to be completely honest you are incredible in bed. Had I known about your sexual prowess you wouldn't have needed alcohol to seduce me."

Trace grinned.

"Does that mean we can hook up again?"

"Yes. I owe you more than one night, but even if I owed you nothing I'd want to hook up again."

Trace's grin broadened.

Our waiter came. Trace ordered Egg Rounds Benedict and I order a Bonne Femme Omelet made with bacon, onions, and potatoes. We both ordered coffee.

"Your parents must be really rich," Trace said. "That's an incredible apartment and your BMW, damn!"

I was tempted to tell Trace the truth, but I needed to keep up my masquerade for my own protection.

"Yeah, they're rich. All my expenses are paid. I get a huge allowance and have a big bank account. I'm taking you shopping after breakfast."

"You don't have to do that."

"I want to do that. As I said, I value my life very highly and *you* saved it. If you didn't want to be spoiled you shouldn't have dialed 911."

After breakfast, Trace protested all the way to the mall. I pulled him into Abercrombie & Fitch, but he still didn't want me to buy him anything.

"We're not leaving this store until I spend a thousand dollars on you. If you want to have sex with me again you'd better start shopping," I said.

"That is blackmail I cannot stand up against," Trace said.

"I know." I grinned wickedly.

Trace and I began to browse. I picked out the hottest sales boy and asked him to help us. The two of us double-teamed Trace and suggested things for him.

"Here," I said, handing him a blue Henley that matched his eyes.

"This is way too small," Trace said.

"Trust me. Go put it on and come back out."

"Yes, sir!"

We waited only a few moments and Trace reappeared. Two girls who were shopping stopped and stared at Trace. The sales boy said "Damn!" and then caught himself. The mystery of his sexuality was solved.

"That is hot," I said. "Everyone in the store wants to fuck you right now."

Trace looked in a mirror.

"It does look good. Doesn't it?"

"Trust me. I know about fashion and looking good."

"I can't argue with that," Trace said, looking me over.

"Are you guys...boyfriends?" the sales boy asked.

"Not exactly," I said.

I leaned over and whispered some of the things Trace and I had done the night before and this morning. Our sales boy blushed and I could see a bulge forming in the front of his pants. He looked back and forth between Trace and me, probably picturing us naked together.

"You'll look good in this color," I said, handing Trace another shirt. "Oh, you have to have this one, and this one, and this one."

I kept grabbing things, holding them against Trace's chest, and then either putting them back or handing them to Trace. The sales boy took the growing stack, carried it to the counter, and returned.

"If you see anything you like, grab it," I told Trace.

Trace was too overwhelmed to pick anything, but I loaded the sales boy down with everything I could think that Trace might want or need, including cologne.

"Hmm, anything else?" I asked, looking around.

"I think you bought everything," Trace said with a grin.

"I guess that will do for now."

We followed the sales boy with the last load and with the help of another sales boy he rang up our purchases, folded them, and put them in large Abercrombie & Fitch bags with shirtless young hunks pictured on the sides.

"The total is $1,873.82," the sales boy said.

Trace's mouth dropped open. I swiped my American Express through the machine on the counter. Trace wandered off in a daze.

We left the store moments later, loaded down with bags.

"Let's take these to the car before we shop some more," I said.

"Shop more?"

"We haven't been to Hollister yet," I said.

Trace's mouth dropped open.

We stuffed all the bags into the BMW and I handed Trace a small slip of paper.

"What's this?" he asked.

"Ben's number."

"Who is Ben?"

"The hot sales boy in Abercrombie & Fitch."

"*He* gave me *his* number? He was hot!"

"It shouldn't surprise you. You're cute and sexy, Trace. I think he's curious to discover why I think you're so hot in bed."

"Wow," Trace said. He stood there just staring at the number. "Wow."

We returned to the mall and did some damage in Hollister, American Eagle, and Areopostale. When we were once more back in the BMW, Trace just sat there looking overwhelmed.

"I have never had anyone buy me so much stuff before," he said. "I've never had so many incredible clothes before."

"You should have thought of that before you saved my life. All actions come with consequences." I smiled.

"You *really* shouldn't have."

"I tend to do whatever the hell I want," I said.

"I can tell, but I still feel guilty."

"You saved my life. Remember? Besides, I have loads of money. I can easily afford to buy you all this stuff."

"Thank you," Trace said.

"No. Thank you!"

Trace had class soon so I drove him to his dorm and helped him carry all the bags from A&F, Hollister, and the other stores we'd raided. I gave him a lingering kiss right in front of his roommate, then walked back out to my car.

I drove my new convertible around town, but my mind was more on Trace than my new car. I liked him quite a lot and not just because he was so very good in bed. I could find good sex with little difficulty, but Trace was fun to spend time with when we weren't naked. I had enjoyed buying him all those clothes. It had given me the same feeling that I'd experienced when I presented Gene with a check that would probably change his life. All my life I'd been adept at spoiling myself, but doing things for others made me feel good inside. It was a unique sensation. I felt giddy and silly, but I didn't care.

I was being quite ridiculous, but then I'd never been a terribly serious person. I'd been aloof, as Trace noted. I'd been selfish and cruel. All things considered, ridiculous was a change for the better. I had done horrible things, but I was beginning to turn things around. I had never been all bad. I had been kind to others at times, even generous. My kindness and generosity was usually self-serving. It was usually a means to an end. Not always. There was good in me. Even when I was doing despicable things to Evan, I was still capable of acting towards others with kindness. It was hard to reconcile the Dorian that used a straight boy with the Dorian who flirted with not-so-hot girls to make them feel better about themselves. Did everyone carry such contradictions within themselves? Did rapists and murderers help old ladies across the street? I thought it likely.

I eyed a cute skater-boy as I drove slowly past. He was young, sixteen perhaps, but rather sexy and cute. I imagined offering him a ride and seeing how far I could get with him to amuse myself. I frowned. Old habits die hard. People were not playthings. I had treated Evan like a toy. I had turned him into an object and now I had to live with the guilt of what I had done. Giving him my car could not make up for the torment, both mental and physical, I had inflicted on him. It's a wonder he hadn't murdered me to put an end to it all. I thought I'd been clever in not pushing him too far, but I had had pushed him *much* too far to be sure. I was lucky to be alive. Had he killed me, it would have been no more than I deserved, but it would probably have ruined his life. I could well be dead now and Evan in prison and all because I treated him as an object that existed only for my amusement.

I looked away from the boy. He was nice eye candy, but he was too young, even if he was willing. I had to establish boundaries for myself and rules. One rule definitely had to be no underage boys. I might look eighteen, but I was old enough to be even an eighteen-year-old's father. I saw no reason for denying myself an eighteen-year-old, but from now on anyone younger was strictly off-limits. It would not be difficult to abide by that rule. There weren't that many boys under eighteen who captured my interest. They just didn't have what I desired. I had hooked up with the occasional sixteen or seventeen-year-old in the past and maybe even with a fifteen-year-old or two, but that was the Dorian who did not care about the consequences of his actions. I had seen my true ugliness through the eyes of Daulton and I was determined to change myself for the better.

***

I spent a lot of time with Trace over the next several days. The boy was insatiable. To put it bluntly we fucked like bunnies. My partners were usually powerfully attracted to me but Trace even more so. I repeatedly had sex with him to thank him for saving my life, but truthfully I would have hooked up with him just as much if he hadn't. The old Dorian would have used him and that instinct was hard to deny, but in trying to please Trace and make our time together as pleasurable for him as possible I discovered new joys in love-making I had not experienced before.

Trace and I did much more than have sex. Even a sex-fiend like Trace could only go at it for so long. True, Trace could keep going through two orgasms, but by the third even the little stud-bunny needed time to recuperate.

I took Trace to restaurants all over town. Some were more upscale like DeAngelo's and others, like Opie Taylor's, were quite common. I'd never been a snob about where I ate. My only true criteria was the food. If it was good, I ate there.

Trace somewhat lacked culture. I don't mean he was ignorant. One didn't get into Indiana University by being stupid. I don't mean he was uncouth either. Like many students at IU he had never taken the time to visit the IU Art Museum, which had a fine collection of not only art, but antiquities from Greece, Rome, Egypt, another many other cultures. He'd never attended a performance in the IU Auditorium. There was so much right under his nose that he had not taken the time to appreciate. I took it upon myself to introduce him to the culture of Bloomington.

I found myself holding Trace's hand across the table more than once. I thought of him often when we were apart. I passed up opportunities with other very attractive young men, even those I wanted quite badly.

I took Trace's hand again as I sat across from him in a booth in the dark interior of the Trojan Horse.

"We've been spending a lot of time together," I said. "Perhaps we should think about getting a little more serious."

Trace smiled, but his smile was rueful. It was not what I expected.

"I don't think that would be a good idea," he said.

"Why? I don't know about your feelings, but I feel very close to you. I think...I think I'm falling in love with you."

Trace shook his head.

"No, you're not. You just think you're falling in love with me."

I looked at him quizzically.

"I know you're a player, Dorian. You pick up guys and then discard them on a whim. I'm not saying there is anything wrong with that. I think we all do it. We're young and horny. We hookup and then we move on. Maybe we come back and hookup with the same guy again, but each hookup is disposable."

"I don't think of you like that."

"I know. Something has changed you. The most obvious answer is the attack. Something like that could shake up anyone's world. I don't think you've ever slowed down enough to truly spend time with someone before."

"I have, but...it's been quite a while and that didn't work out so well."

"Have you ever been in love?"

"Yes, but..." I couldn't tell Trace the truth. Even if I dared I couldn't tell him about Caleb. "I was in love, but...he died."

"I'm so sorry," Trace said.

"It's been years, but..."

"You must have been *very* young then," Trace said.

I realized then I'd slipped.

"I was fifteen," I lied. "I loved him very much." That was no lie.

"How did he...no, I'm sure you don't want to talk about that. My point is I'm the first guy you've gotten close to. I think you're mistaking friendship for love. We have a lot of fun together. The sex is incredible and all the rest is great, too, but it's not love, Dorian. You don't really love me. You care about me, but as a friend. I feel the same way about you."

I sat there, feeling suddenly depressed. Was Trace right? I thought for a few moments. Was I trying to recreate what I'd once had with Caleb? Had I latched onto the first guy I could and fooled myself into thinking I loved him?

"I don't want to be your boyfriend, Dorian, because I don't want to get hurt and I don't want to hurt you either. I'm not ready to stick with just one guy. I'll be honest, I'm too much of a slut for that and Bloomington is one big smorgasbord of hot boys. You are the most beautiful of them all, but my eyes would rove. I could lie and say I'd be faithful, but I know I don't have it in me. Even if I could, I don't believe you love me. If I let myself get too close you'd hurt me."

I started to protest, but Trace held up his hand.

"I don't mean you would hurt me on purpose, but I'd get hurt just the same. You would realize you didn't love me and that we'd make better friends than boyfriends. You would want to stop dating and *that* would hurt me, even though it would be the right thing to do. We are best as friends with benefits."

I sat there playing with the silverware, thinking that Trace was probably right. I felt like I loved him but what he said made a lot of sense.

"I've been trying to change myself. I've been trying to be less of a jerk and a user. Maybe I'd trying too hard. Maybe I'd trying to rush into a relationship so I can feel like I'm making progress."

"Could be. I think you're succeeding. We've been spending a lot of time together and I haven't noticed you being a jerk once."

"That's because I owe you my life."

"No. I mean with others. I've seen you doing nice things for others when you didn't know I was watching. You know what I'm talking about. I'm sure you haven't become a nice guy over night, but you are different. I stalked you before the night of that party. I set my sights on you and was determined to have you. I watched you and I followed you. I witnessed some things that...well, let's just say that part of the attraction was that you were a bad boy. You were merciless and dangerous. You could be rude, arrogant, spiteful, and downright malicious. I'm not saying you were evil incarnate, but you were not a nice guy. Even when we hooked up at the party, you used me and didn't look back. True, I seduced you, but the second you shot your load you forgot all about me. I was nothing to you. I haven't seen any evidence of that since the night of the attack.

"Since that night you've been different, Dorian, and I'm not talking about all the stuff you've bought me. You have changed...or are at least changing. I hope we can continue as friends and I definitely want the sexual benefits to continue, but you don't really want to date me, just as you don't really love me. You just think you do."

"Why can you see all this so clearly when I can't?"

"I'm older."

I rolled my eyes. If he only knew...

We had a nice meal and I drove Trace back to his dorm. I couldn't help but feel the sting of rejection. It was an emotion I was not accustomed to. If there was rejection, I was the one dealing it out. I wasn't sure about what Trace had said, but in at least part of my heart I knew it was true. It was as if I knew it without knowing it. I guess it didn't matter if I believed it or not. Trace did.

I parked the BMW by the stadium, but I didn't walk straight back to McNutt. I wanted to walk and think and so I wandered aimlessly around the stadium, Assembly Hall, and on up 17th Street past the outdoor pool.

I felt lost, alone, and sad. I'd made so many mistakes in my life and the biggest of all was with Caleb. I'd told myself a thousand times his death was his fault, not mine, but I knew it was a lie. I had been merciless and cruel and now I was alone because of it.

I sighed. At least I'd finally woken up to what I was and what I was doing to others. Not so long ago I would probably have enacted some nasty revenge on Trace for rejecting me, but I didn't even consider it now. If anything, he had done me a favor by speaking the truth. He had risked losing everything with me to keep us both from getting hurt. I felt no malice toward him in my heart. That was a good sign.

I walked down to Kirkwood Avenue and then west. I ended up in front of The Kirkwood. On impulse, I went inside. I entered my apartment and made straight for the study door. I had not entered the room since the night I'd come so very close to murdering Daulton.

I turned the key in the lock and entered. I flipped on the lights. There stood the life-sized, framed portrait hidden under black satin. I pulled the cover away and gazed at Dorian, at myself, at my own soul.

The Dorian staring back at me was in his mid-forties. His hair was thinning and wrinkles were forming around his eyes and the corners of his mouth. His skin had lost the smoothness and beauty of youth. It was all as it should be.

A smiled curled up the corners of my mouth. Dorian's eyes had lost much of their cruelty. The expression on the face was no longer filled with malice. There was a sadness to the eyes, an expression as if the evil side of Dorian was mourning its own demise. That more than anything gave me hope.

The lustfulness of the gaze was still present, but it had lost most its leering quality. The disdain had faded as had the hatred and contempt. None of these things had been eradicated and perhaps they could never fully be erased for this was truly me. None of us was without sin. I was very pleased, elated even, at what I saw reflected in this mirror of my soul. While the Dorian who gazed back at me didn't exactly look kind he was not too terrible to behold. Certainly, there was much work to be done yet, but I had made a start.

I covered the portrait once more for it had to remain a secret between Daulton and myself. I do not know what power created its ability to bear my age and the evidence of my sin, but no one could be allowed to view it for no one would understand. I say not that the portrait bore my sin, for it did not. I had learned that it only bore the physical evidence of my sins. I bore the sins myself, as everyone bore theirs, they merely weren't reflected on my countenance.

I turned off the lights, closed the room, and locked the door. I left my apartment and walked back toward McNutt and my life as a college boy. I smiled. I had made a good start.

Epilogue

Daulton finally returned after six months in Paris. We had kept in touch by post card and phone, but it had been far too long since I'd seen my old friend. Paris had been a success. One of Daulton's works had been exhibited in the Louvre and his star had risen. I couldn't have been happier for him.

I sat in Daulton's studio as he told me about his trip; the museums, the wine, the food, and the artists. I listened eagerly to his tale, but also impatiently for a question to pass his lips.

"I've been going on and on about myself, Dorian. I've forgotten to ask how you have been doing. You look wonderful, but then you always do."

"Come with me and I'll answer your question," I said.

I led him out of the studio and to my own apartment. I ushered him into the study and uncovered the portrait.

"This is how I've been doing," I said, standing back and grinning.

Forty-something Dorian gazed at us, but all sign of malice and evil was gone. There was a certain wicked mischievousness to the glint of his eyes and in his smile, but there was no rancor or ill will.

Daulton turned to me, smiled, and hugged me. When he released me, we stood there and gazed at the portrait together.

"This is how I'm doing and you are always welcome to come and check up on me by looking upon the Picture of Dorian Gray. You shall be my second conscience, Daulton, so that I shall never trod the dark road again."

The End

Listed in suggested reading order

Outfield Menace

Snow Angel

Ancient Prejudice Break to New Mutiny

The Soccer Field Is Empty

Someone Is Watching

A Better Place

The Summer of My Discontent

Disastrous Dates and Dream Boys

Just Making Out

Temptation University

Someone is Killing the Gay Boys of Verona

Keeper of Secrets

Masked Destiny

Do You Know That I Love You

Altered Realities

Dead Het Boys

This Time Around

Phantom World

The Vampires Heart

Second Star To The Right

The Perfect Boy

The Graymoor Mansion B&B

Shadows of Darkness

The Heart of Graymoor

Yesterday's Tomorrow

Christmas in Graymoor Mansion